I0648758

George F. Herrick

An Intense Life

A sketch of the life and work of Rev. Andrew T. Pratt, M.D., missionary of

the A.B.C.F.M., in Turkey, 1852-1872

George F. Herrick

An Intense Life
A sketch of the life and work of Rev. Andrew T. Pratt, M.D., missionary of the A.B.C.F.M., in Turkey, 1852-1872

ISBN/EAN: 9783337299439

Printed in Europe, USA, Canada, Australia, Japan

Cover: Foto ©Raphael Reischuk / pixelio.de

More available books at **www.hansebooks.com**

AN INTENSE LIFE.

A SKETCH OF THE LIFE AND WORK OF

REV. ANDREW T. PRATT, M.D.,

MISSIONARY OF THE **A. B. C. F. M.,** IN TURKEY.

1852——1872.

BY GEORGE F. HERRICK,

OF ANATOLIA COLLEGE AND MARSOVAN THEOLOGICAL SEMINARY

"I must work the works of Him that sent me while it is day."

:: Fleming H. Revell ::

NEW YORK :   CHICAGO :

12 BIBLE HOUSE, ASTOR PLACE.   143 AND 150 MADISON STREET.

= Publisher of Evangelical Literature =

NOTE BY REV. GEORGE WASHBURN, D. D., PRESIDENT ROBERT COLLEGE.

The following sketch of Dr. A. T. Pratt comes from one who was intimately associated with him in his last years, and is well qualified to appreciate his character. There was nothing in Dr. Pratt's life which was startling or sensational, but it was an inspiration to all who knew him.

When, in the weariness of controversy, I seek for a living demonstration of the truth and power of the Gospel, his life is one of those which always comes up to confirm my faith.

I commend this sketch to all who are praying and working for the redemption of the world, and especially to those young men in our colleges and seminaries who have consecrated themselves to Christian work, at home and abroad.

GEORGE WASHBURN.

Robert College, Constantinople.

INTRODUCTION.

Hands that could better have prepared this sketch **have** either been laid to their last rest, or are too burdened with work to admit the undertaking. The sketch was partly written before the extreme paucity of material from the sources thought most likely to afford it in abundance was fully known. It is hoped that the record, brief as it is, will stimulate many youth in their resolves and aspirations toward that only life worth living, a life of usefulness to others.

To the writer himself this renewed association with one of the rarest spirits it has ever been his privilege to know, has been emphatically, a labor of love.

The following is from a minute adopted by the Mission to Western Turkey, at its annual meeting in May, 1873.

"Resolved, 2.—That we record our grateful acknowledgement, that, in God's good Providence, our Brother Pratt was spared to do, for twenty years, most efficient work in a greater number of departments of missionary labor than has, perhaps, been the privilege of any other missionary, viz.: Direct and even pioneer missionary work, the administration of missionary responsibility in connection with the work in its advanced stages, the instruction of a native ministry, the translation of the Bible, the general work of the Press, and the work of a missionary physician.

" Resolved, 3.—That our departed brother was permitted in God's good Providence, to an unusual degree, to leave behind him the record of success all along the line of his missionary life, and that the hopes and plans he cherished, including the last darling purpose of his heart in connection with the work he laid down when called up higher, have been realized, or bear the sure pledge of their realization, while, from the first to last, our brother's native modesty and Christian humility remain in memory as a singularly bright example.''

It is surely fitting that one of whom such judgment can be put on record, should live in the memory of those that come after him. It is the judgment of those who knew Dr. Pratt best, that a brief sketch of his character and work cannot fail to be a healthful stimulus to those who may read it.

Our brother's life might almost be said to have no earthly record. Evidently it was never in his thought that he had any other record to make than that of deeds well done and a consecrated life worthily lived. Besides his official reports to the society that sent him out, few of his letters are to be found ; his journals were mere jottings, nothing personal. Many of those to whom he wrote most frequently, in the earlier years, have, like him, joined the company who serve God day and night in His temple. In later years his letters were few. Dr. Farnsworth, of Caesarea, has kindly allowed the writer access to a full correspondence of his with Dr. Pratt, covering more than half of his missionary life ; and several facts stated in this sketch are based on those letters or comfirmed by them. These give repeated evidence of the dangers attending upon travel in Turkey, and of the annoyances and sometimes real suffering incident to such travel and to the lodging places. but these are matters well known, and years of experience render one indifferent to most of them, and improvement comes with time even in Turkey.

No attempt is made to write Dr. Pratt's biography.

We simply pause, for a few brief moments, in our own life conflicts, to glance back over the race, swiftly run, of a servant of God, to catch inspiring glimpses, here and there, as amid an Alpine landscape, of an intense life, all directed toward the highest ends; of a devotion that conferred too little with flesh and blood; of a life that had, to human prudence, too early an ending.

The senior Aintab pastor says:

"Although he lives no longer in the flesh, yet he lives in the hearts of those who knew him."

And another friend:

"In this world we shall see his face no more; 'He hath fallen on sleep,' but his memory will be fragrant for long years to come."

> "So he who blesses most is blest,
>   And God and man shall own his worth
> Who toils to leave as his bequest
>   An added beauty to the earth."

CONTENTS.

––––

THE SKETCH.

I.

Andrew Tully Pratt was born of pious parents, at Black Rock, near Buffalo, N. Y., February 22, 1826.

The family subsequently removed to Berlin, Conn., where, in 1837, when eleven years of age, Andrew was received into the Christian Church. A little incident of his childhood well illustrates that physical and moral sensitiveness that characterized him through life. When but four years old, on one occasion, in his father's absence from home, his mother conducted family prayers, and prayed for each of her children by name. When the family rose from their knees, little Andrew said: "Mother, when you pray for me, it hurts me here," striking his hand over his heart; "right here." He was led by his mother, who long survived him, to look forward to the ministry and the missionary work, almost from the date of his conversion.

He commenced study, preparatory to a liberal education, at the Academy of Berlin, with his eye

upon the work to which he subsequently devoted his
life. Throughout his long course of preparatory,
collegiate, theological, and medical studies, he uni-
formly did the best work with the least noise. His
power of acquisition was much above the average;
his progress was both sure and rapid. "I never
knew his equal," says a classmate, "in improving
every moment of time."

Another classmate writes: "I knew him well and
had a very high admiration of his character. He
was one of the most sincere and guileless persons I
have ever known, one whose Christianity was of the
very heart and soul of the man. I think the missionary spirit was born in him very early and
amounted almost to a passion."

We gladly insert the following reminiscences given
by Rev. W. E. Moore, D.D., of Columbus, Ohio:
"Dr. Pratt entered Yale College, a freshman in 1843.
He was then in his eighteenth year, but in appearance far more youthful. His fresh, ruddy countenance, his flaxen hair, and his undeveloped stature
gave him a boyish aspect. But his manliness and
true dignity of self-respect won for him the regard
of all, and marked him as one who would be an
honor to his class. His preparation had been thorough, and it was obvious to all that he had come
to college with high and manly aims. He was universally known to his classmates by his middle

name, Tully, and the name Tully Pratt, was a title of endearment to those who knew him best.

"It was my privilege to be intimately associated with him in class division during our whole college course, and to share the hospitality of his home—then in New Haven—in no stinted measure. From the beginning of the course, he stood high in scholarship and was blameless in conduct, a model of regularity and punctuality in attendance upon all college exercises. If he had any preference in his studies it was for the classics, but his scholarship was remarkably uniform. A most conscientious student, with a high sense of duty, he resolutely mastered whatever task was assigned him. He made large use of libraries in his leisure hours. His reading, outside of the immediate studies of the class, was chiefly history and biography. In the Junior and Senior years he developed mentally with great rapidity. At graduation he stood within the first six or eight in a class of 124, many of whom have since become distinguished.

"He entered college a professed Christian, and was always known as an earnest and consistent follower of the Master. He was always present at the prayer meetings of the class and college, taking his part in the exercises. His piety was not fitful nor emotional, but it was known to all to be the controlling guide of his daily life. His leading characteristic was a quiet but intense earnestness, which showed itself in everything he did. By nature he was modest and unobtrusive, but he never shrank from what seemed to him to be duty. Duty with him was imperative, and he always undertook it with confidence in the Divine guidance and help. He was a young man of remarkable purity of speech and behavior; no one ever heard from him an impure word or saw a doubtful act.

"From the beginning of his college course he felt strongly drawn toward the work of Foreign Missions. When he graduated, after years of conscientious self-scrutiny as to his motives and his fitness for that work, and of careful preparation for it, his purpose was fixed to enter that work, should God call him to it. His was the enthusiam of a deep and earnest nature; with high and holy purposes, fed by familiar communion with God, and deepened by the ever-growing conviction that he was called to glorify God in the work of the ministry, whether at home or abroad.

"His college life was the sure prophecy that whatever God might call him to do, he would do it with his might, and with success. His missionary life— to human view all too brief—was the fulfillment of that prophecy. Few of our missionaries have been more deserving to be held in everlasting remembrance."

Young Pratt graduated, in due course, in 1847, and, in the five years following, completed, at New Haven and New York, a full course of theological and of medical study. Throughout his course of study, he received but a small modicum of aid from his father, not more than a thousand dollars, largely supporting himself by teaching and other work.

A classmate of Dr. Pratt in the New Haven Theological Seminary, has kindly supplied reminiscences of his later student life from which we condense what follows:

"Among the choice spirits whose names, to the writer, are fragrant with the sweetest memories, is the late Dr. Andrew T. Pratt. Beautiful and simple were the elements that made up his social life. Some years ago, when a good man died, one said of him: ' those who knew him in private life will naturally recur to his admirable social qualities, the frankness of his disposition, the generosity of his sentiments, the largeness of his views, his extraordinary conversational powers, his perfect independence, and yet courtesy in differing from others.' These words may be applied to Dr. Pratt. Socially, ' he spread his joy over all the day,' ' a man of cheerful yesterdays and confident to-morrows.' His intellect was one of high order; he was a keen observer; books were his companions; he was eager to enrich his mental culture; yet, in reading, he re-

membered the saying of Carlyle; ' If time is precious,
no book that will not improve by repeated readings
deserves to be read at all.' In the seminary class of
1852, no one read more or better books than did
Young Pratt. His was a life of prayer in its best
and highest meaning. He talked with God as friend
talketh with friend. When Moses had been talking
with God, the skin of his face shone, but he knew
it not. No more did our brother realize the light
and blessedness reflected from his own soul life.
Others saw and were constrained to say, ' How beautiful are the ways of one who keeps near to Christ;'
and in those praying circles, when in that upper
room, a few of us met once or twice a week, what
voice more sweet, and tender, and mellow, with
the love of Christ than his of whom I write."

"I cannot forget his pleadings, so gentle and yet
so earnest, that the Life which was, and is, the Light
of men, might take possession of all our hearts.
Of all the young men at that time in the Divinity
School at New Haven, I do not recall one who, in
my judgment, had in him more of that spirit which
prompts its possessor to pray without ceasing.

"His aim and end in life was to exalt Christ. He
could say, in all sincerity, ' I am crucified with
Christ, nevertheless I live, yet not I, but Christ
liveth in me.' Christ to him was real. He looked
into His eyes; he took hold of His hand; he walked

by His side; he joyed in His presence; and when
he left home and friends that, in a far away land,
he might be the beloved physician both to the bodies
and the souls of men, it was the love of Christ that
constrained him."

———

II.

THE VOYAGE—THE MEDITERRANEAN—SYRIA.

Dr. Pratt received his appointment as a missionary of the American Board, and was designated to
North Syria, now the Central Turkey Mission, in
1852, was ordained August 8, the same year—married the same day to Miss Sarah F. Goodyear—and
on the 22d of the following December sailed from
Boston for Smyrna, in the bark Sultana, together
with Rev. (now Dr.) W. A. and Mrs. Farnsworth,
Miss Maria A. West and others. It was not till
several years later that sending out missionaries
by steamer was even thought of by the officers of
the Board. "The long sea-voyage is an admirable
time for reflection," Dr. Anderson used to say. And
if there was, in any case, too much of romance in
the setting out, it was liable to be cooled amid the
experiences of the sailing ship! And yet those
little cabins were very Bethels oftentimes, witnessing renewed and complete consecrations, close and

sweet Christian communings of kindred minds, and fruitful efforts for the salvation of seamen.

The voyage was unu..ually short, only thirty days from Boston to Smyrna. The associations formed on the Sultana grew into life-long friendship, especially between those who lived and worked long together either in the same mission, or in those adjoining; those who used a common language and labored chiefly for the same race, meeting similar experiences as the years of life and labor passed.

Miss West says: "Dr. Anderson kindly placed me under the special care of Dr. Pratt; he had said to me that they had never yet sent out a man so thoroughly qualified for his work in both the Theological and the Medical Departments. An own brother could not have been more kind, considerate and thoughtful for a sister's comfort and welfare than was he then and even up to the time of his departure for the 'Better land.'"

In the early days of the new year, the Sultana passed the Pillars of Hercules, and the Rock of Gibraltar, the old home, on either side, of Spaniard and of Moor,—on into the clear, blue waters of the Mediterranean. Every bay and headland, every rood of shore, the very sky and air are full of stories of the ages of the peoples that have made up human history. There are few men in whom both soul and sense would keep time more accurately, to the

music of such environment than was true of Dr.
Pratt. A few days—and his nerves thrill and his
blood tingles as he looks on the near hills of Greece,
passes among her islands, catches a glimpse of the
Temple on Sunium, and even sees, in the distance,
the very acropolis of immortal Athens. There is a
witchery in the very clearness and softness of the
still air of early morning. Again and again has he
crossed already the track of that Apostle to the
Gentiles, in whose footsteps he is literally to tread
in the coming years. He disembarks at Smyrna,
and his feet press the soil trodden eighteen centuries before by the "Beloved Disciple," and one
century later by his pupil of like spirit, the noble
Polycarp. "Infidel Smyrna," the Turk calls it, because the Christian population has always greatly
outnumbered the Moslem. He reads ancient inscrip-
tions, visits historic sites, but his soul goes out to
the people, and his work. His mind is busy—his
heart beats quicker with the thought, "this land is
henceforth to be my home; these people, Greeks,
Armenians, Turks, are those whom I am to learn
to love henceforth, whose salvation I am to seek, in
whose tongue I am to tell of a living and loving
Savior."

At Smyrna Dr. and Mrs. Pratt separated from
their missionary traveling companions, and embarked on board a steamer which took them along

a coast in whose every line he read the history of
Ionian Greek, and of Christian Greek, of twenty-
five and of fifteen centuries ago.   He passed by
Ephesus, Rhodes, Cyprus, and landed at Alexan-
dretta, to begin his missionary life close by where
Paul embarked on his first missionary journey. He
was now nearing his future home, Aintab. Only
the land journey of less than a hundred miles remained.

The whole region into the centre of which he
thus came, in the ardor and passion of a missionary
devotion never excelled, seldom equalled, is a region
crowded to bursting, with historic memories and
ancient relics. About thirty-eight centuries ago,
the feet of Abraham, the "Friend of God," passed
over that very soil, from northeast to southwest.
About sixteen centuries later, over those lands, on
either side of the Euphrates, Alexander the Great
had rushed, like a sirocco, to his glorious conquest
of Persia, and his inglorious death at Babylon. In
the following years the same region was the centre
of the Syrian or Seleucian monarchy, a fragment of
that vast empire that Alexander had conquered
but never formed, much less ruled. Over Roman
military roads, still traceable, the Roman legions
passed and repassed in the decades before and after
the birth of Christ. In the middle centuries of our
era, Armenians had pushed southward from their

REV. A. T. PRATT, M.D.   19

ancient homes, and lived in those storied lands. Four
and a half centuries ago, the ruthless Tamourlane
had there wantonly slaughtered his helpless victims
in hecatombs and myriads.

Nearly every form of the civilization of the ancient
world successively had its home in those fertile
lands, and lastly the Turk swept northward and
westward from Central Asia and trampled on them
all. Dr. Pratt was the very man to be deeply impressed by such surroundings, and it is one of the
striking evidences of his devotion to a high purpose,
that while the relics of ancient history attracted
his attention, and were observed with intelligent
interest, his references to them, in what he wrote,
are always brief.

III

THE ARMENIAN PEOPLE.

It is, at once, a wonder of history and a triumph of
Christianity, even when that Christianity is cor-
rupted, that two and a half millions of the Armenian
race still exist, after six centuries of oppression, and
not only exist, but show a wonderful elasticity and
capacity for intellectual elevation and spiritual reno-
vation. Through a large part of North Syria and
Anatolia, the Armenian race almost wholly lost
their national language, and were forced to adopt

that of their conquerors and oppressors. Yet it is
pathetic to see how they have clung to some words
of their own language, salutations, words expressive of Christian ideas, proper names, etc.

The writer, not long since met with an intelligent
Armenian community in a Turkish city, the members of which are ignorant of the commonest words
in Armenian, and yet are quite offended if one, not
a Moslem, bid them, "Good morning," or "Good
evening," in any other language than their own national tongue.

At present there is an enthusiastic revival, in all
the principal centres of the Armenian population,
of the study of their national language.

It was among this race that evangelical influence
in North Syria, as in other parts of Western Asia,
gained the first strong foothold under the labors of
the American Missionaries, which began at the capital, Constantinople, twenty years before Dr. Pratt
came to Aintab, a city of North Syria of some
35,000 population, about one-third Armenians and
two-thirds Mohammedans. He reached that city
March 2, 1853, when the work there was—we may
say—a little more than five years old. He was ap-
pointed to take the place vacated by the death of
the lamented Dr. Azariah Smith, and to be associated with the well known missionary, Rev. Benja-
min Schneider. D.D.

IV

THE FIELD AND THE NEW LABORER.

The work in Aintab itself had already gained considerable momentum, and was well started in other places; but there was not yet a native ministry, not even a single native pastor. In the work of education only a beginning had been made. The Gospel had been effectively and eloquently preached, and with marked results. But the great work of establishing permanent, growing Christian institutions, whose seed is in themselves, institutions ecclesiastical, evangelistic and educational,—the slow process of remolding society and establishing vital Christianity, the new birth of races, the inauguration of a new era which is now well begun,—all this solid foundation work was then future. In this Dr. Pratt had a large share.

He entered upon his work, as regards every form of preparation, exceedingly well equipped. But above and beneath all other equipment, he had,— one might almost say he was one intense and dominant purpose, viz.—to offer to the Master, in all simplicity and humility, the largest, the richest, the completest possible service, till life should end. Whatever he was, whatever he had acquired, was consecrated, without reserve, to the service he was entering. Beneath those flashing eyes, in that little physical frame, lay coiled up a tremendous spirit force. From that time on, for twenty years, that force glowed like a furnace of anthracite; it burned like an electric light. He went right into the harvest field, all ready for the sickle, and we may say that he wielded a sickle in each hand, as he was both doctor and preacher. How earnest— how plaintive they appear to us now—the calls he made again and again, during those early years, for reinforcements. No general ever held a position or made an advance with higher determination, with truer heroism, or with clearer consciousness that he was very rapidly spending and being spent in the struggle.

V

ACQUISITION AND USE OF THE LANGUAGE.

Dr. Pratt had hardly set foot upon the soil of Turkey before he began the systematic study of the language, the Turkish, which he so soon and so signally made to serve his one life purpose. As a physician he had his hands full of work from the beginning. At the same time, there were multitudes on every hand ready to hear the message of salvation from his lips. Under such a pressure, most men would have been content with very moderate attainments in the language. Not so Dr. Pratt. If a dragoman may not blunder in interpreting between the embassador of his sovereign and the ruler to whom he is accredited, he was unwilling to blunder in telling the message of the King of Kings to high or low, to the learned or the unlearned. He acquired the language thoroughly. He used the best helps that books could give him; he talked with men of every rank and race. In this respect his position as a physician gave him access and scope not within the reach of all. And after the first years,—we might, in his case, almost say the first year, had passed, his use of Turkish, in conversation, in preaching, in teaching, in official communications, oral and written, in his printed books, both in prose and poetry, was marked by transparent clearness, correctness, force. He effected no elegant tricks or meretricious blandishments of style—too common in native writers—but the common man knew his meaning, and the learned Turk gained new respect for his own language when he heard it from this foreigner. Turks wondered at his use of their language, and sometimes could hardly be persuaded that he was not a native of the country.

VI

EARLY MISSIONARY EXPERIENCES—MEDICAL PRACTICE.

As said above, Dr. Pratt reached Aintab March 2, 1853. On the 28th of the same month he wrote:

"The work here and in the neighborhood is truly great. The American Churches do not begin to know what it is, or to appreciate the want of men. Hardly a sermon is preached but we hear of some impression made by it. There are other places nearly as interesting, though the work has not advanced so far."

Just six months before, Dr. Schneider whose life and work has made so deep a mark upon that whole region, had made his first visit to what has now, for many years, been one of the great evangelical centres of this empire, viz., Marash; and that visit may be regarded as the real beginning of the great work there, the first foothold gained against the fierce persecution with which the Gospel was first received, a persecution more sharp and persistent, perhaps, than at any other point in the land.

Dr. Pratt wrote to Mr. Farnsworth April 23.— "I am fairly at work practising: go to the dispensary every day for an hour, have had 150 different cases." A little more than a year later he says: "I have now students who can make up my medicine prescriptions, and as I am free from 'making pills' myself, I don't mind the number of patients."

At one time there were seventy persons arranged in three rows around the doctor's study. Three years later the assistant accompanied Dr. Pratt to a neighboring city, and under his personal inspection, opened the eyes of thirty blind people by performing the operation for cataract.

The oldest Anitab Pastor, Rev. Krikore Haratunian, states that one of Dr. Pratt's medical pupils has performed 2,300 successful operations for calculus and more than 3,000 other surgical operations. Many years later, while residing on the Bosphorus, and in enfeebled health, his friends tried to persuade him to use some of the fees received for medical services among the English residents near by, to purchase a horse and so secure needed exercise. His unvarying reply, "my time, my strength all belong to the American Board; this money is not mine," shows that the devotion of his early years was the conscientious rule of his whole life. An incident taken from his correspondence with Dr. Farnsworth, in the year 1854, shows what was the significance of his work as Missionary Physician. In September of that year, there was severe sickness in the family of Mr. Ford, of Aleppo. The doctor went to Aleppo, with Mrs. Pratt, to be absent from home several weeks. They were, without doubt, the means of saving at least one life. Dr. Pratt says: "Brother Ford threw the responsibility on us, and so, I think, was saved from sickness himself. It is pleasant to be useful. I didn't do much else at Aleppo, only wrote one sermon a week!" (The exclamation point is ours, not included in the quotation). Those who

know by experience what the doctor's position must
have been, will wonder that he found a free minute
to write out even the text of a sermon at such a time.

The following is from a letter of Dr. Pratt, dated
April 28, when he had been on the field just eight
weeks, and when his associates, Mr. and Mrs. Crane,
were compelled, for reasons of health, to retire from
Anitab: "On account of Mr. Schneider's absence on
a tour to Diarbekir, Mr. Crane preached all day. In
the afternoon he addressed the people for the last
time. When he had finished nearly all were in tears.
It was thought it would comfort the brethren, as I
was to be left alone with them, if they could see me
take some part in the service. I read from the third
chapter of John. Seldom has one had an audience
more in sympathy with him. I felt a new joy, and
when one of the brethren prayed for him who had
then first read to them from the Holy Scriptures,
tears of joy and thanksgiving came, that even so
feebly, in such a place, I might make known the Gospel of Salvation. To plead with them from a free
tongue will be precious work indeed. It seems to
me that this missionary life is one of high joys and
keen sorrows; and one of the keenest sorrows is to
feel that these poor people who are earnest for instruction must be left to their ignorance, because
none can be found to come and teach them or those
who are here are called away."

Very early was our brother called to drink of this cup of sorrow, of which he was to drink so often and so deeply in later years.

In his letter of July 30, Dr. Pratt mentions the constant interruptions, sometimes needless, upon his hours of study, of those who came for medicines, etc., and various other annoyances incident especially to a missionary's earliest experiences, and says:

"Mr. Dunmore, the indefatigable missionary pioneer in Eastern Turkey, while alone at Harpoot, some year or more ago, found his time taken up with calls and conversation with inquirers of every description. He had not yet learned his famous, laconic answer, a single word in Turkish,—to questions merely curious: 'It has not been written.' Under the pressure he resolved to seize upon some time, each morning, for preparing his sermons, and gave notice from the pulpit accordingly, carefully noting the hours when he desired not to be interrupted.

"The following morning, just as he had opened his Bible, there was a rap at his door. He gave his visitor, one of the principal men of the congregation, rather a cold welcome, saying: ' Didn't you hear the notice and request I gave yesterday?'

"'Oh, yes,' was the reply, ' and that is why I came now; I knew others would be deterred from coming,

and so we should have time for a good long talk all
to ourselves!'

" You must not suppose from this that we are disheartened. I only mention these facts as part of a
true picture. Disheartened! Oh, no! If the people
are wanting in certain things, we wonder that they
are as correct as they are, when every appearance
of prosperity is only a signal for new burdens and
taxes. We rejoice at their willingness to learn; we
wonder that anything is left to a people oppressed
by foreign rulers and debased by their own church.
When we see, as we often do, sweet Christian experience, with the fruits of love and peace and other
Christian graces, we give thanks to Him who has
wrought these things by his mighty power. And
when we see evil passion, and wrong in the heart
and life, we yearn over the subjects, and rejoice that
we are here to live and labor for them. We do love
the people and the work, and desire no higher office
than this ministry wherewith we minister."

VII

IN HARNESS.

When Dr. Pratt had been at Aintab barely eight
and a half months, and that the hot season of the
year, with time for study much interrupted, he went,
unattended, except by native companions, to the

then new field of Marash, to engage, for nearly two
months, in the most intense sort of missionary work.
It is doubtful if this has any parallel in missionary experience; a tour like that undertaken, and a
language as different as the Turkish successfully
used, after eight and a half summer months in the
field. As Marash was, in later years, Dr. Pratt's
home, a few words of description may fitly be given
here.

The Taurus Mountains are that grand range,
which extends from near Brusa, running nearly
south to within fifty miles of the Mediterranean,
then east, almost to Harpoot, dividing extreme
Western Asia, Greek Asia, or Asiatic Hellas, from
Anatolia, the land of the "Sunrising," and then
Anatolia from North Syria. What was afterwards
known as the Marash Missionary Station occupies a
section of the Taurus range, including more than
6,000 square miles, and is a region of grand natural
scenery. Seen from a high point near the centre
of the range the mountains seem piled one upon
another.   ·

The city of Marash, about forty miles north of
Aintab, with a population of 30,000, one-third
Armenians, lies among scattered foot hills, which
skirt the base of the southernmost ridge of the
Taurus. The houses are so scattered that not more
than half of the city is seen from any one point.

Back of the city the mountains rise 4,000 feet above
the sea, 2,000 above the city. Opposite the city, toward the south, is the mountain which forms the
abrupt terminus of the Amanus range, which runs
north from Mount Lebanon, and the valley at the
south and east may be regarded as the northern
limit of the "Entering in of Hamath," since it con-
nects, at the south, with the valley of the Orontes,
and so with the region of Coele Syria.

Dr. Pratt's own words shall describe his work at
Marash, on the occasion of his first important tour.

VIII.

REPORT OF THE VISIT TO MARASH, 1853.

"Marash, November 18, (day after arrival), I had a
visit from about ten persons.

"Sunday, 20.—We have had three services. The
one at eight o'clock in the morning was most fully
attended. Twenty-eight men, eight boys and three
or four women were present at Sabbath School.

"Sunday, 27.—Our largest number to-day has been
twenty-nine.

"30.—To-day I was building a new but rough room
for my better accommodation, when I was agree-
ably surprised by my wife's appearing, in company
with a much esteemed native brother. I had more
cause for thankfulness than I knew, till I heard her

account of the fearful scene through which she had passed, and how the Lord had delivered her out of the hand of violence.*

"What renewed obligations we are under to devote these lives to his service!

"December 1st.—We are quietly settled in our own board palace, ten feet by twelve. An old woman, a Protestant, insists that she will bring us milk every day. Has she not served the old Church these many years, and never got any good to her soul? Now was it a great thing to do something for those who brought the Gospel to her? She told us she had

---

*Dr. Schneider had accompanied Mrs. Pratt half the distance from Aintab; they had been beset by robbers and roughly handled. Mrs. Pratt, however, was not ill-treated, only greatly frightened.

Few missionaries of experience in Turkey have escaped falling once or more, into the hands of robbers. Three missionaries have been killed by robbers within thirty years, viz.: Mr. Coffing, Mr. Merriam and Mr. Parsons. Perhaps none have failed to meet with robber bands on their journeys, or to see the gleam of their weapons, from behind some shelter to right or left, when they have been restrained from attack by Him who guardeth His people from the terror by night and from the arrow that flieth by day. Such incidents sometimes have both an amusing and instructive side.

Dr. Goodale, of Marash, was once traveling with one attendant when three suspicious looking and heavily armed men joined him from a road on the right. He stopped to lunch; they stopped, too. Soon they began to boast of their arms, and come to close quarters. It was before the day when all robber bands were armed with the best revolvers. Missionaries generally go unarmed, but Dr. Goodale, carried a good six shooter. "Pooh, your arms are nothing," said the Doctor. "See here," and deliberately discharged, one after another, three of the barrels of his revolver, careful to reserve as many charges as there were robbers opposed to him. "And it will keep right on so, and, see here," he said, and pulled out his false teeth and held them up. Suddenly the robbers bade the foreign necromancer good bye and turned and went on their way.

Mr. Dunmore was once traveling, unarmed and alone, when he was stopped by two mounted and armed Koords. They

feared God all her life and been very faithful to the
rites of her Church; but she never could find peace
till she found it in the pure Gospel of Christ.

"December 4th.—Sunday, forty-five different hearers.

"December 5th.—I have been called to-day to see
a sick priest. His case is not hopeful as to any expectations of his recovery; but I talked with him
freely on spiritual and personal religion, and the
blessed privilege of going directly to Christ, rather
than to saints and creatures. He did not interpose
a word of objection. I was afterwards called to two
other priests, and had similar conversations. There

demanded his money, but he had so very little that they said,
with a manner that made them appear terribly in earnest, "Now
we are going to kill you." "Very well," said Mr. Dunmore. "I
came here to preach the Gospel to such as you; let me preach to
you first, and then you may kill me," and pulled out his New Testament and began. They were awed by conduct so extraordinary,
and let him go unharmed.

Rev. J. W. Parsons, the gentlest of men, at least twice met with
robbers before that last waking from sleep for one brief instant,
on his quick passage into heaven. Once he was returning from
Constantinople to his home at Bardesag, with a donkey load of
books, mostly New Testaments in several languages. As he was
passing through the stunted trees below his house, he was
stopped by the notorious Sefteri, a Greek, the terror, for years, of
the shores of the Nicomedia Gulf. The sum of money that Mr.
Parsons had with him was but a few piasters, and the robber was
going to take the load. "The load is all New Testaments, and
there are some in Greek, and the price is six piasters, you had
better buy one," said Mr. Parsons. Whether Sefteri thought it a
good joke, or from higher motive, he bought a Testament and
sent the missionary safely to his home.

On another occasion Mr. Parsons, together with his wife and
Miss Farnham, was returning from a tour in his field when,
rounding a corner in the road, he was suddenly brought to a halt
by a man pointing his gun at him. The man got but three dollars, after all his searching, and complained: "Now, this isn't
fair; I've waited, day after day, for a week, right here, for your
return, and now am I to get but three dollars?"

were present from five to ten persons at each place, who thus heard the truth, with a confession of it from' their own teacher. I find, however, one difficulty in talking with many of the people. They have a vague, supei stitious religionism, which trusts alike to Saints and to Mary and to Christ; and when you speak of the Savior, they astonish you with expressions of the most perfect trust and deep Christian feeling, while we must often think that all is heartless and vain. Sometimes, however, they profess they do not know, and show by their manner that they do not care.

"December 8th.—I have been left, contrary to my expectations, without help for nearly two weeks, and find that I suffer from holding six services a week. But what can I do? After service this evening I felt unable to move; but soon I had a call from some half dozen persons to discuss a question about baptism, and I could not refuse them. So it is, a missionary is placed where there seems to be no way but to overwork; and then the churches wonder that he breaks down. If they would man every post, they would not see their men thus cut down so often.

"December 31st.—I went to-day with Mrs. Pratt to the last of seventeen families which she has vis· ited since her arrival. They have received her kindly and listened to her reading and remarks.

"January 1st, 1854.—Our year has begun with the

largest audience we have yet seen numbering in all sixty-six, of whom fifteen were married women.

January 2d.—Our school is daily increasing, having now twenty-five in all.

"January 3rd.—When we parted with some who followed us out of the city, their last cry was: 'Do not forget to send us a missionary;' and I went on my way, musing sadly in my heart, for I did not know who would go. I will take up the cry and send it over the waters to you. I cannot send them a missionary, cannot you?"

Dr. Pratt returned to his post and work at Aintab in the first days of the year.

IX.

KESSAB.

Kessab is a village with a population of 2,000 Armenians—no Moslems—situated at the head of a fertile valley in Mount Casius, south of Antioch and near both to the city and the sea. The high, bare, precipitous rocks of the mountains behind the place are its citadel. The Gospel gained a strong foothold there early, and the progress was rapid; it was an out-station of Aintab. In midsummer of 1854 we find our brother taking his vacation, as missionaries very commonly do, by one of these tours "in the field," which brings a missionary into the most vital and constant touch with the people in their own homes. He visited Kessab, where persecution was then raging, a long report of which he made to the Missionary House, and by means of which the good work made rapid progress. Of another visit to Kessab, made nine months later, i. e., two years after he reached his field, he writes thus:

"On the Sabbath before I left we had a very solemn communion season. The room was crowded as were the windows, and even a neighboring roof, with attentive listeners. I spoke of the agony and death of Christ, and after receiving the confession and covenant of the new members, administered the simple rite. It was intensely interesting, and a remark of an Armenian who was present for the first time disproves the argument of those who say that shows and pageantry are necessary to impress rude minds. He had seen the mass a score of times, but he said, after witnessing our simple service, that he had never seen Christ crucified so plainly before. In the afternoon seven children were baptized, and the house was again crowded. To my sermon on baptism, a plain exposition of its nature and meaning, they listened with a serious stillness that was very gratifying. The day, as a whole, was one of the most interesting that I have ever spent; and it was closed by a few words of advice and encourage-

ment to the brethren who came to my room in the
evening. No one could fail to have his heart warmed
by such a visit."

————

X.

OORFA—A NEW CHURCH.

In the autumn of the same year, 1855, Dr. Pratt is
found on a tour eastward to Oorfa, as medical and
preaching missionary; and, although the place was
not yet occupied as a station, hardly as an out-station, yet he had the satisfaction of forming a Church
in that ancient and important centre, "Ur of the
Chaldees," as missionaries in that region have generally held it to be, is a city of nearly 40,000 inhabitants, about one-fourth of whom are Armenians or
Jacobites, the latter numbering about a thousand,
situated in Mesopotamia, half way between Aintab
and Mardin. It has always been a place of impor-
tance, and, since 1857, has become an important
evangelical centre. Dr. Pratt says: "On the second
Sabbath of December, we were permitted to form a
little Church of six members, five of them males and
celebrated the ordinances of Baptism and the Lord's
Supper. This is the first time that this has been
done, in a Scriptual way, for hundreds of years. It
was a most interesting occasion, and the hearts of

the new communicants were very tender. We trust
the faith of Abraham has once more revived in the
home of his childhood."

———

XI.

UNDER PRESSURE—REGRET.

Reports and preserved accounts of Dr. Pratt's work
grow less full as the work he did became more mul-
tifarious and pressing,   acquired experience making every skilled blow tell with more decisive significance, while his strength to meet the too heavy
strain grew less. His medical knowledge and skill,
his sound judgment, the thoroughness of his intellectual training, his strength of will, his utter freedom from all vacillation, either of mind or character,
his facile use of the language, his quickness of exe-
cution, made him a man constantly in demand.

Already we anticipate the keen regrets, strongly
expressed by our brother in his later years: "No
man should attempt to be both a medical and a
preaching missionary; he will inevitably fail in one
or both, or break down in his prime." He never
could quite give up medical practice, as he would
gladly have done; and even after his health failed,
he would go anywhere, at any time, at any degree
of personal sacrifice, to render medical service in a

missionary family, or to those in need and without
other help—his kindness ever more precious even
than his skill—and certainly he did break down early
from excess of labor.

The extract that follows is from a letter of Dr.
Pratt to the Missionary House, dated February 23,
1857, when he had been on the field not quite four
years. His senior associate was absent. Perplexing difficulties had arisen in the Church, in connection with their own affairs, in connection with the
support of the Head of the Protestant Civil Community at Constantinople, and in connection with a
movement to establish Episcopacy in their midst.
The labor, and still more, the burden of responsibility, thrown upon a young missionary, must have
been fearful. The first native pastor had been ordained less than a year; i. e., in March, 1856.

"The past year may be said to have been one of
unbroken prosperity among the people in all their
temporal concerns; and recently, their credit has
been increased by the deposal of a bribe-taking Gov-
ernor, directly in consequence of their representa-
tions at Constantinople. You will readily believe
that all these things have had no little influence, and
that, too, of a kind not the most desirable. Worldly
prosperity and honor, the success of almost all their
plans, both private and public, continual additions
to their numbers, and the universal respect they com-

mand, are working, I fear, that love of the world, that pride and self-consequence to which the human heart everywhere is so prone. But perhaps, in all this, there hath no temptations taken them, or us, but such as is common to man. We are embarked in a large ship, we have a fine breeze, and are making good headway; but for all that, there are breakers here and there, and be the helmsman as skillful as he may, if the crew do not work with him, the vessel may go ashore. And so, too, it may, if the pilot mistakes and fails to steer right; but we hope for better things.   .

"We have much cause for gratitude for the degree of harmony existing between pastor and people, and for the relief we have ourselves experienced from his aid. Though the taxes of the people have been heavy, they have collected, besides the pastor's salary, 4,000 piasters for schoolhouse and school; 1,800 piasters for an addition to the Court of the Church, and 1,740 piasters for the poor and the heathen. Our average audience has been 670. Native women have taken up Mrs. Schneider's work among women, since her death. We have counted 272 women who can read, 80 of them still connected with the Old Church. Our book sales have been increased: prejudices among the Armenians are breaking down." In the same letter Dr. Pratt gives account of a believing Turk, and reports a recent hopeful tour to Kessab.

XII.

ALEPPO ET UBIQUE GENTIUM.

Dr. Pratt removed in October of this year, that is, 1857, to Aleppo, the capital of the Province, the most important commercial centre of Asiatic Turkey, a worldly and wicked city of some 80,000 inhabitants of many races, mostly Mussulman. Till 1855 it was a part of the Syrian Mission, and was occupied by a missionary; the chief languages are Arabic and Turkish. He nominally resided there till the spring of 1861, when he joined Mr. Morgan at Antioch, that great centre of the Christianity of the first centuries, when the disciples were first called Christians—present population about 15,000, and lived in Antioch till his removal to Marash in 1863. We say "nominally," because he resided at the out-station, Killis, almost as much as at Aleppo, and he was frequently called to other stations or out-staions, as the needs of the work in the whole mission required. For example, he was hardly settled in Aleppo before he was called back to Aintab, to assist in settling the difficulties referred to in the above extract from his letter. After that visit he wrote as follows:

"In looking back we see great gains from this unprecedented confusion.

1, "'We have the whole matter of the Head of the

Civil Community fully understood by all the people, a thing vainly striven for before, for more than three years.

2. "'We have their confession of ability and their promise to pay, and to render it obligatory upon every member to bear his proportion of this burden.

3. "'The position and relation of the pastor are better defined and his influence increased.

4. "'We have tried, and proved to be sound, the moral sense of the mass of the people.'

"However many adhered to the opposing party for a time, it was not from any unwillingness to do their duty in the matter, but from an undefined fear of some tyranny to result from this relation to their Cival Head. This fear removed, they were on the side of right. The hold the pastor has on the affections of the people was also manifested. The women, especially, were very zealous, and one proposed to get two hundred women to subscribe and pay the whole amount."

————

XIII.

RAPID PROGRESS AT MARASH.

In October, 1858, at the close of a letter written from Marash to the Missionary Home, on "Sanitary Topics," Dr. Pratt says: "I can hardly help alluding to our visit here nearly five years since, and to

the great work God has done in that time. On the
Sabbath nineteen were received to church fellowship, making the whole number ninety-six, all gathered in four years. I saw a sea of six hundred faces
before me; five years ago the most was sixty-six.
The community now numbers nine hundred souls;
then it was less than forty. What a work to be en-
gaged in!" Yet he says in a private letter some time
before: "I do not much rejoice in large congregations—long for a deep spiritual work."

XIV.

LITERARY WORK.

From about this time on, till his visit to America,
early in 1860, Dr. Pratt spent a part of his time,
associated with Mr. Morgan, in preparing, in Turkish, a brief text book of Systematic Theology. The
book was issued from the Mission Press at Constantinople in 1861, and is a 12mo, of 264 pp.—
nominally a translation from an English original.
But in fact Dr. Pratt spent much labor on the book;
and as Christian Theology in Turkish was well
nigh a terra incognita, a careful writer would be
compelled to "turn back his stile " continually. The
work is one of real merit, and did much to keep
the evangelical churches "steady " in the fierce

storm of controversy over the Atonement and kindred doctrines, that broke out in the Central Mission and raged so threateningly between the years
1865—1867. Dr. Pratt always claimed that the
book would have been many per cent. better if it
had not been so much "revised" by the Publication
Committee at Constantinople, "to suit the style of
the Capital." As very high authorities claim that,
of places in the empire, Aintab takes the palm in
the matter of pure idiomatic Turkish, and as, con-
fessedly, among foreign Turkish scholars, Dr. Pratt
never had a peer in the province of Aleppo, it is
highly probable that his judgment on the "revision"
of his Theology was not far wrong. Certainly, as
time passes, Turkish style at the Capital is more
influenced by the best usage of the provinces.

XV.

ALBUSTAN AND YARPUZ.

In the Autumn of 1859, Dr. Pratt made an ex-
tended and important tour through his own "field"
and nearly the whole of the Marash field.

He says, in reporting his visit at Killis: "There
has been a great increase of interest and the number of Mussulman hearers is quite considerable.
Every Sabbath as many as five men and women

and oftener ten or fifteen, are found listening to
the sermons."

The report of the visit to Albustan and Yarpuz,
lying north of the Taurus, cannot be very much
abridged: "We were soon over the mountains, and
all day were in the pine woods of the northern slope
of the Achur Dagh, till at night we encamped on
the banks of the Jihan. Our tent did good service
in a rainy and cold night. Early in the morning
we entered the pass of the Taurus, through which
this rushing river finds its way, and all that day
were creeping along precipices on narrow ledges, or
clinging to the sides of steep hills. Once, on our
return, a pack horse, missing his footing, fell down
one of these narrow paths and was instantly killed.
The scenery was grand in the extreme; rock upon
rock, frowning precipices, one after another, almost
endlessly, and the river running at the bottom of
the valley in maddest fury. When about nine hours
from Marash, we came to the bridge on the Zeitoon
road, burned some weeks since by the Zeitoonites,
when the Pasha led an expedition against them,
for the sake of compelling them to pay large ar-
rears of taxes, an attempt in which he was unsuc-
cessful. Some twelve hours from Marash, under
a threatening precipice, on the right bank of the
river, are the forges of the Zeitoonites, for fear of
whom no Protestant has heretofore been able to

pass over this road. I am happy to say that I met
with neither injury nor insult, and esteem this as
one sign of the softening down of this bigoted people. (A large number of these bold Armenian moun-
taineers have since become earnest, evangelical
Christians). On Friday, the 7th, we turned off
from the pass, and crossed the mountains, and our
rain became snow. We had exchanged the summer
we had only three days before, for a cold wind in
our faces, and a heavy snow-storm for two hours.
We suffered but little, however, and on Saturday,
the 8th, we arrived at Albustan."

XVI.

VISITORS.

"The next day, besides the Protestant brethren,
all of whom came to see me, I had two calls from
Mussulmans. One was an old, and poorly dressed
man, who immediately asked me to read. I opened
where I had just been reading, and we were soon
discussing the meaning; I had many a talk with
him afterwards. He was once in comfortable cir-
cumstances, but some years ago began to seek salvation, gave up his business and lives now on a
mere pittance. He now appears even to accept
Christ as God, sacrifice and Savior, but has many

crude notions about 'denying the flesh,' about
'dwelling in love,' and 'dying to the world.' Half
mystic, half ascetic, he is not, I fear a Christian and
perhaps never will be.   I had calls during the week
from ten Mussulmans,   all of them talking freely
about our doctrines. They acknowledge Christ's
divinity, and some of them speak quite boldly.
They are rather heretical Moslems, than Christian
inquirers, but their well-known sentiments and
their uniform approval of Protestantism gave an
opportunity for labor among this class of people
which is scarcely found in any other place in
our field.   One young man, not connected with those
mentioned, has been, for a year or two, under the
influence of the truth. He seems to be a renewed
man, avoids sin, is conscientous, and keeps the Sabbath. Many know of his position, but as yet he
lives in peace; may he be the first fruits of a great
harvest. A Moslem priest of much repute, took
one of our brethren aside one day, and asked him
if there would be any protection for him if he should
preach Christ. He had obtained a New Testament,
and had read it with some care. Doubtless he is
not a solitary instance of such secret conviction,
and some day—who knows how soon—the whole
land will be open before us, and we shall be called
to go in and freely offer the benefits of evangelical
Christianity to all its races.

The third week, after examining candidates for
Church membership, and accepting three, I spent
three days in visiting Yarpuz. This is a village
of some 350 houses, 60 of them Armenian. It is the
ancient Arabissus (Yarpuz is not Turkish, but a cor-
ruption of the ancient name), once, as scores of col-
umns testify, a large place. I found one Greek
inscription on a tombstone, and others had evidently
been erased; but, strange to say, many a Moslem
grave had an old headstone adorned with the cross.

XVII.

ALEPPO REPORT, 1860.

In the spring of 1859, the state of Mrs. Pratt's
health made it necessary for her to leave the field
for a time. Her husband accompanied her across
the Mediterranean, and thence returned to his post,
leaving her, with little Clara, to go on without him.
He followed his family a year later, and closes
the report of his station, April, 1860, as follows:

"We thank God for the work in Killis, and take
courage for Aleppo. It is a worldly and wicked
city, but needs the Gospel all the more for that;
and we are willing to spend and be spent for it, if
it be God's will concerning us. It is important in
itself and important in its relations, and we hope

will not be left unoccupied. We commend it to the Mission, trusting that the best possible provision may be made for it, and leaving it to Our Heavenly Father, to place us here again, or not, as may seem best to Him."

XVIII.

LIFE AT MARASH.

While still occupying the Aleppo-Antioch Station, in the late autumn of 1862, Dr. Pratt visited Adana, and had a share in the early stages of the work in that important centre. The failure of the health of both Mr. White and Dr. Goodale left the important Station of Marash vacant, and Dr. Pratt went there to reside in 1863, and did there, perhaps, the most important work of his life, whether as preacher, teacher, author, or guide in missionary affairs. There his own health broke down. While there he buried his beloved daughter, Clara. There he watched over the swift and fatal illness of his younger and stronger associate, and most promising missionary, Rev. Zenas Goss, who died August 28, 1864. From there he went for rest, in 1865, only to have the beloved Morgan removed from the work they labored in together. There he gathered in the fruits of a most powerful revival. There he taught in the School of the Prophets, and prepared men of like spirit for the work of the ministry.

From there he made his last removal to Constantinople to engage in the work which was in hand
when he received his final and early release from the
ranks of the Church militant. When he went to
Marash, to reside, he found the Protestants there
in unhappy condition, unworthy men in the Church,
and divisions occasioned by youthful ambitions
fostered by outside support. This state of things
soon gave place, however, to a prosperity which has
continued till the present time. About this time he
wrote: "It does not do to have all our work suc-
ceed; we get to be too large; our plans must fail
that God's may be carried out."

XIX.

A DANGER AVERTED.

A much greater danger threatened all the churches
of that region in the year immediately succeeding,
which Dr. Pratt did more than any other man to
stem and, in the end, completely to avert. The
missionary who occupied the Station of Oorfa from
1859 on, had developed certain pronounced views on
the fundamental doctrine of the atonement, which,
if not positive errors, as held in his own mind, were
in apparent opposition to the doctrine as held by the
Board and its other missionaries in Turkey; and,
as time passed, as was not unnatural, a party was

formed that laid great stress on these peculiar expressions of doctrine. The missionary himself also
made it a matter of conscience to defend the posi-
tions he had taken. The greatest peril of all lay in
the unquestioned fact that this missionary was a
man of great earnestness and signal success in his
work. Extensive and prolonged revivals had taken
place under his ministry. All this was calculated
to give prominence, almost to glorify the new form
of presentation of doctrine, and the personality of
the leader. His warmest partisans claimed the results of his work as the legitimate fruits of his peculiar views, and to oppose a loved and successful
missionary brother, and yet not harm the work and
the Church of Christ was no easy task. Dr. Pratt
took prominent part in this controversy, supported,
happily, by such men as Dr. Schneider, Mr. Morgan
and Mr. Powers; he formulated clear, scriptural,
unpolemical statements of doctrine; he was charit-
able and patient; he urged to unity and forbearance;
he was conciliatory in all minor matters; he left his
own personality out of the controversy; he admirably
illustrated the "fortiter in re," united with the "sua-
viter in modo." With such a winning example,
coupled with firmness in what was essential, others
were persuaded, and by 1868 the danger had passed,
the harmony of the churches was preserved and
sound doctrine universally accepted.

XX.

ZEITOON.

Two more extracts from letters of Dr. Pratt's from Marash should find place here. The first is of date July 28, 1864:

"You know that it has been, for years, impossible for any Protestant, much less for a preacher of the Gospel, to visit Zeitoon (the mountain stronghold of Armenian robbers, who long successfully defied the government, and we have longed for an opening by which we might visit it. Last year, one of Dr. Goodale's medical students went, and one of our helpers; but after a few days a mob took them from their beds and drove them out. This, however, was progress from former times, and prepared the way for our visit. Last month one of the principal men of the place, being sick, sent to his partner here, who is a deacon of our Church, begging that I would go and see him. My family was not in good condition to be left, but such an opportunity was not to be missed; so with two Zeitoonites and the medical student mentioned, I started a little before noon. The road is very rough, and we took two long rests; this brought us to Zeitoon late, and over a road so bad that the guide said, in one place, I had better not dismount. The horse was used to the road and would pass it more safely than I could. I thought so too, as, in the moonlight I looked down the slipь.ery sleep. We reached the house about midnight. On the way, our guide had pointed out the places where, in the summer of 1862, the battles were fought between the Turks and the Zeitoonites; and the morning after our arrival our host showed us from the roof of the house, the position of the Pasha, his cannon and the various troops. A great change has come over Zeitoon. This is manifest not only in the fact that we could go there so freely, and walk the streets unmolested, or sit in the market and talk as we did, no one hindering; but also in the fact that, for a year past, there have been no local quarrels. The people themselves say, ' we are not as we were.' Every man and boy had his pistols at his belt; and often, over trivial matters, blood was shed, as a few years ago over a matter of four piasters. Now, for a year, no such thing has occurred, and some there seem to desire this state of things. There has been, for some months, a new society of 'The Enlightened' among them, who meet every Sabbath, and have an exhortation from the Scriptures from one of their number; they are opposed to wine-drinking, and breaking the Sabbath. We visited at one house, the entire membership of which are evangelical, if not Protestant. In the house of our host we had morning and evening prayers, attended by several from outside."

The other extract is from a letter of Jan. 12, 1867.

XXI.

THE REVIVAL OF 1866-7 AT MARASH.

"I take advantage of this letter, though driven with work beyond my strength just at this time, to tell you of the good hand of the Lord with us in these few months past. The spring and summer were made memorable by the death, often sudden and unexpected, of many young and prominent members of our community and Church. We saw no outward signs of the Spirit's blessed work, but now, as for more than a month, the examinations for admission to the Church have been going on, new evidences of a deep work have been daily afforded us, and we are constrained to lift up our voices of thanksgiving, while bowed in the dust for our own faithlessness and coldness. Our prayer meetings have been gradually increasing in numbers and interest, and this week of prayer has been a very jubilee. Both churches have been opened an hour before sundown, each day, and in each a gathering of two hundred and fifty or more has attested the interest of the people, while the offering of ten or fifteen prayers, two or three rising at once, and the pastor's vain endeavor to close the services, in less than an hour and a quarter or an hour and a half, show that the coming was not a mere form, and made us sensible of the presence and power of the Holy Spirit.

But it is to the examinations that I wish especially to refer. In the First Church there were fifty-two candidates and twenty-nine were received. This is a very unusual number to receive; i. e., twenty-nine out of fifty-two; and the character of the examinations was more remarkable than the number received, as attesting, with startling vividness, the power of the Spirit to change the heart and life. In the Second Church they have examined about forty, and received twenty-one or two new members. Some of the cases I know to be of great interest."

XXII.

THE YEARS OF CHOLERA.

1. IN 1865.

While still residing at Marash, in the summer of 1865, Dr. Pratt went to Constantinople for a season of rest, "leaving Mrs. Pratt," as he said, "to do my work for me in caring for the poor and the sick." It was the year of the great visitation of cholera at the capital. Our brother gave much time to visiting the sick, and still more, in giving to others stronger in health than he then was, specific directions how to treat cases. There is no doubt that he was the direct means of saving very many lives, for the disease, that year, though rapid and violent, and though its victims were numbered by tens of thousands, yet yielded to a remarkable degree, to prompt remedies, faithfully used. It needed the backing of a competent and cool-headed physician to give us the courage to apply, without hesitation, the heroic remedies sometimes successfully resorted to. He was a guest at a Missionary Home on the Bosphorus. Mr. —— came home one day from the missionary headquarters with heavy tidings.

2. A SUDDEN BLOW.

Rev. Homer Morgan, at this time Dr. Pratt's most trusted and experienced associate, had died of fever at Smyrna, while on his way to the United States, as suddenly as Mr. Goss had died less than a year before. Dr. Pratt took in the full significance of the terrible news in an instant. It meant a great loss to the mission. It meant loading shoulders already sadly bending under their burden with a double load. He knew it would crush him. He reeled under the blow the news gave him; he sank down; he almost gasped: "Oh! brother——, pray." After that prayer he prayed, and how he prayed! The recollection of that hour is very vivid in the memory of his companion.

It probably saved him from a final breakdown then that he was obliged to make a brief visit to

the United States to accompany the bereaved family
to the home land.

3. IN 1871—DEATH OF LITTLE ANDREW.

The visitation of cholera at Constantinople, in
1871, was very different from that of 1865 in respect
to yielding to remedies, although its ravages were
not so great. Dr. Pratt was then residing in a very
healthful location on the height of Roumeli Hissar, on the Bosphorus, a village which wholly escaped the scourage in 1865. First, a Scotch servant,
a Christian girl, in the family of Dr. Pratt, and then
his little son Andrew fell victims to the disease.

In the case of the child especially, the disease
not only defied all remedies, but was so rapid
that his nearest missionary associate, informed in
the early morning that little Andrew had been taken
with cholera about midnight, had barely time to
hasten to the bedside of the sufferer soon enough to
to watch with the stricken parents the last half hour
of life. When the last breath was drawn, the father
put his hand upon the child, and said: "He is gone,"
and turning to the agonized mother, said: "Oh!
Mother, I've no doubt he, at this moment, is just as
happy as he can be." How swift the rising from
what the eye of sense could see to the clear vision
of the heavenly rapture. Not even the father himself
could go to the child's burial, which was, of course,

hastened to avoid infection, and was attended only by a missionary associate and two native assistants. How often that fine-strung soul was called to bear the loss of children. Six several times, the trial came, and one more child has followed him. How happy the group already gathered in the Father's House. The chronological order of events has here been intentionally disregarded; and we return to speak of the last unfinished chapter of the life and work of our beloved brother, viz., his work as a

----

XXIII.

TRANSLATOR OF THE BIBLE.

In 1867 it became the general sentiment in the Central Turkey Mission, where the popular version of the Bible in Turkish was most widely used, as well as among the Churches, that the version must be revised to meet the change in language—or rather the people's use of it—then rapidly taking place. Dr. Pratt was plainly the one man for the work. It was evident that he could not long hold out under the strain that came upon him in the mission where his work had been hitherto done. Such a revision could be best undertaken at the Capital, the great centre not only of political and politico-ecclesiastical, but also of literary influence in Turkey, where the work of the Press of all the Turkey Missions is done—the city of unrivalled beauty of site, a city so crowded with historic monuments that it is a marvel that many educated travelers come to Southeastern Europe and yet turn westward without setting foot in the city founded by Constantine, the home of Justinian and Belisarius, the city of Ecumenical Councils, of revolutions in government, the city of Christian and of Moslem glory, of Saint Sophia and of the Mosque of Solomon, the magnificent —the city of Chrysostom. But the pen must be stayed. It is no part of our present duty to describe Constantinople, the Golden Horn—the Bosphorus, on whose European bank Dr. Pratt lived the last four and a half years of his life, to recall the life of Chrysostom and the Gregories, the Latin or Moslem conquest, or to give glimpses of the seething human life of that scattered metropolis of the East, with its million people, composed, as the Turks say, of "the seventy-two and a half nations of the world."

WIDE REACH OF THE PLAN.

From the hour of decision to go to Constantinople for the work of Bible revision, Dr. Pratt had ideas more far-reaching than those which were the ostensible object of undertaking the revision. As a physician, he had been thrown much among Turks of all classes, and he knew that while in former years,

Turks used a purer and perhaps higher style of language than the Turkish speaking Christian races, yet education was now making much more rapid progress among the Christians, especially the Protestant Christians, of the Aleppo Province, than among the Turks. Moreover, if Turks had the advantage over their Christian neighbors purely in the matter of language, still Biblical thought is familiar to the Christian and foreign to the Turk. Therefore once granted the necessity for a pure and correct Turkish style for the growing demands of Turkish speaking Christians, and there could be no reason why the same style should not meet the wants of Mohammedans also. And if there were no valid reasons against the unification of the versions, there certainly existed the most cogent reasons for it. One of the standing objections urged by Moslems against Christians, especially Protestant Christians, is that we deal in the freest manner with the text of our Sacred Book, and they know not what our Bible is. This fact renders it our most solemn duty to make one and but one version, and that, as far as possible, a perfect version for all who speak and read Turkish. When we have one version, in whatever characters printed, in clear, pure Turkish that all can understand, and that the most sober Turkish scholarship will approve and endorse, we have gained immensely in the massing of all our

Christian forces for the conquest of all races for
Christ; we have opened the door of salvation more
invitingly to the Moslem races, and greater is the
multitude who welcome Moslem inquirers to the Living Fountains in the identical words of a common
Bible. There are twenty million souls whose ver-
nacular is the Turkish. No difficulties, no personal
preferences, or interests or judgments, nothing must
stand in the way of the accomplishment of a plan
so beneficial, if its accomplishment can be brought
within the sphere of what is practical.

A LIVING GERM.

Such was Dr. Pratt's thought. Would others
share it? Would the demands of Constantinople
Turkish style justify his idea? Had others similar
ideas? Dr. Pratt brought to Constantinople, in
March, 1868, a Turkish grammar which he had prepared on the basis of the well-known grammar of
Fuad Pasha, and which was still in manuscript—
it **was** printed and put into circulation the same
year. He read over the whole of this grammar to one
of the Turkish speaking Missionaries in Constantinople, thus comparing notes, in detail, in regard to
the sort of Turkish required for the Mohammedan
and the Christian races. His idea received ready
endorsement, and that unexpectedly strong and em-
phatic. And although the idea was not formally

adopted by the Mission and the Bible Societies while Dr. Pratt lived, yet from the hour when the reading of that manuscript grammar was finished, that idea was a living germ, bound to grow and ex-pand. Its fruit is now filling the land. While Dr. Pratt lived, he was, ostensibly, revising what was known as the Goodell version of the Bible in Turk-ish, in the Armenian character. He always had a singular fondness for the Armenian character to write Turkish in, inexplicable except on the ground that coming when he did to Aintab, he first learned and used that character. It grew to him and he grew up in it. Of course he read the Osmanly char-acter freely, but he always wrote Turkish in the Armenian character, and preferred to read it in that character also.

In his work of revision he was assisted constantly by Rev. Avedis Constantian, formerly pastor of one of the churches at Marash, later a member of the Committee for revising the Scriptures in Turkish, and at present member of the Publication Commit-tee, and also of the General Press Committee at Con-stantinople. He had the advice of Osmanly critics, one of them being of very high rank and fame. He was assisted also by the veteran translator and ori-ental scholar, Rev. Elias Riggs D.D., LL.D., with special references to the original languages of the Bible, and to secure uniformity, in sense, of the

new version, with other versions of the Bible, especially in Armenian and Bulgarian, used alongside
of the Turkish version in the Ottoman Empire. He
was also assisted, for a part of the time, by Mr.
Herrick, now of Marsovan. Before Dr. Pratt's death
he had published his revision of the New Testament
in Armenian characters (it actually issued from the
press after his death), and had made much progress
in the revision of the Old Testament. His work
was of the greatest value to those who came after
him. The style adopted by the Committee to whose
hands the whole work was subsequently intrusted,
is much nearer that of Dr. Pratt, than to that of any
previous version.

Miss West reports the following incident as illustrating his spirit in translating the Bible, and as a
commentary on the verse—"If any man lack wisdom
let him ask of God.' "I was an unnoticed listener in
a corner; Dr. Pratt and his assistant had met with a
sentence which baffled them; finally he said, ' Let us
ask God about it; and both knelt for a moment in
prayer to Him who understands all languages, then
rose and solved the difficulty,

The personal attachment between Dr. Pratt and
his associate, Rev. Mr. Constantina, were very close,
fraternal and lasting.

XXIV.

AS LYRIC POET.

Perhaps there is no sort of pure and precious influence started by our beloved brother more beneficial and perennial than that which comes from the hymns he translated or composed in the Turkish language.

Says Dr. Schneider: "He was fond of music and had not a little of poetic taste. This qualified him to be an excellent hymnologist, and he wrote some original hymns and translated more from the English. Many of the best hymns in the Turkish Hymn book are from his pen; and when a hymn became necessary for some special occasion, he was expected to furnish it. While he is quietly sleeping in the dust, how many will be cheered and quickened, generation after generation, by the strains of his sweet hymns." It is no disparagement to those who labored before or contemporaneously with him to say, and the best living writers of hymns in the language would gladly endorse what is here said, that the high water mark of Turkish hymn-writing was touched by Dr. Pratt in two or three of his best hymns. It is believed that in every quality of a perfect Christian lyric, not in the form of adoration, few hymns can be found in any language superior to the two hymns, quite different the one from the other, entitled, "My

Savior Knows," and "A Momentous Question."
These hymns are sung by tens of thousands, and
will be sung in the coming years, and no congregation ever sings either of them without being deeply
moved. And no wonder. Each was produced in
hours of intensest feeling, when a mind of singularly
delicate mould was most fitly attuned; when a soul,
etherial and aspiring, was passing through the furnace of affliction, heated to a white heat, but holding
on to the hand of Him who walked also in the midst
of the fire. The hymns cannot even be read without
emotion. The first is expressive of the sweetest and
most perfect trust, and the other, in minor strain,
is startling in its unveiling of the emptiness of this
earthly existence, and the infinite gravity of the
issues of life. The language of both is a wonderful
triumph of the most idiomatic acquaintance with
the resources of a noble language, coupled with a
rare skill in making the words just express the finest
Christian thought and feeling. If in any sense
translations they were so completely "fused in the
crucible of the writer's mind, spun out of the very
bowels of his chastened experience," that they were,
in every best sense, his composition. How the soul
of the author exults and triumphs, or warns and
beckons still, in these living gems of lyric poetry.
The only hymn-writer in Turkish who has touched
the same chords with similar mastery of thought

and feeling and language, is one—not a missionary who was for years, in the most intimate association with Dr. Pratt.* Some one has applied this as a test of an immortal hymn, "It had to be written." Dr. Pratt's best hymns will all bear this test.

Some of his translations also, as, for example, that of the hymn "Just as I Am," are wonderful as expressing, without loss, the full and perfect soul of the original hymn, no hint appearing of translation from an Occidental language.

These hymns do not appear with the author's name, and few of the evangelical people of Turkey are aware how much their hymnology has been enriched, for all time, by the rare jewels our brother added to it.

---

*During the years 1873 to 1878, the writer had the rare privilege of intimate acquaintance with one of the most learned Christian gentleman he ever knew, an intimacy fostered by working together over Bible translation,—an Arab Koord, Keifee Efendi by name. In a strange sort of university he acquired that rare knowledge of the Arabic language, of the Koran, of Mohammedan tradition, philosophy, law and science, which made his help in the translation of the Bible into Turkish invaluable.

There is a custom among those Koordish tribes of the region of Mosul, of resorting, from different tribes, far and near, to the feet of some recognized Gamaliel, some Plato, near whom the pupils live, sleep, study and receive instruction, through a course of several years. Their suite of rooms is the open air, their laboratory the mountain stream, their books, in parchment, the heirlooms of the learned of their tribe, the entire impedimenta of each, one long shirt, their food the coarse bread, with an occasional cucumber, in its season, given by the people, as their endowment of the university! Keifee left his studies in the mountains to be a teacher in the city of Mosul; he had found the cover of a Bible in the mountains, the book was destroyed by an Imam—sought and found the Bible itself, at Mosul, was instructed in it by the Mosul deacon Meechah, as the Eunuch was by Philip, or Apollo by Aquila. He asked me, later on, more and more clear

XXV

AS PREACHER.

As a preacher, Dr. Pratt was unmistakably clear, instructive, sympathetic and impressive rather than eloquent and profound. He labored to teach Christian truth, and make needful practical impressions, and in this he always succeeded. It is doubtful if he ever preached "a great sermon;" it is certain he never preached a poor one. He simply preached the Gospel, with directness, and, as attested by results, with power. Some remember occasions, one in particular, at Aintab, when, in times of crises in the Church and community, he held and moved the audience of twelve hundred souls with that power of irresistible persuasion which is the very soul of sacred oratory. His downright and unmistakable earnestness and sincerity of conviction was all the secret there was about it. He preached much, on Sundays and other days, in cities and towns and villages, to great congregations and to single households. He wrote his sermons in full in the first years, but subsequently spoke with greatly increased freedom from a few notes, written either in English or Turkish.

---

cut questions,—the questions of a docile mind,—concerning the Gospel narrative, than I was ever asked by any other person. He grew in Christian knowledge and Christian character, as we worked together over the Divine word. He died within a year after the Bible work was finished. The memory of our fellowship is sweet: it is broken but for a little while."

He once ventured on what I am not aware that any other missionary ever did; he exchanged with an Armenian Bishop. He says the Bishop preached an evangelical sermon for him, and there is no doubt he preached a sermon filled with the very marrow of the Gospel to the Bishop's great congregation. He was at once liberal, and in the highest degree and in the exactest sense evangelical.

A well-known and highly esteemed native pastor and teacher, who knew our brother all his life, thus speaks: "In our mission Dr. Pratt gained high distinction both as a physician and as a missionary, so that any record of his life would be very welcome in the regions of Aintab and Marash. He was a generous, noble, kind man, beloved of all. His leaving Marash was a great loss to us. His memory among us is still sweet and cherished. He had great influence with the Government and with other nationalities than our own. He preached with earnestness, with love and sometimes with tears. I owe being myself led to repentance, to two sermons of his, preached on two successive Sundays, more than twenty years ago. The texts I well remember. I think many others were led to repentance by the same sermons. The texts were: 'I perceive that thou art in the gall of bitterness and in the bonds of iniquity,' and 'One thing thou lackest.' "

Before his removal to Marash to reside, he spent

a winter there, and, according to the testimony of
the best known of the Marash pastors, from whose
letter the above extract is taken, his preaching was
the central visible power of a work of grace, one
result of which was the gathering of between fifty
and sixty into the church.

XXVI

INCIDENTS.

1.—SCENE BY THE GRAVE OF MR. GOSS.

His weight of influence over men, and his tact—
his daring even in seizing opportunities is well
shown in the following incident, reported by Rev.
Avedis Constantian: "In 1864 there was at Marash
a quarrel among some of the brethren, the parties to
which the lamented Mr. Goss had labored hard to
reconcile. At the time of his death, this effort had
not reached success. While the great crowd was
weeping around the open grave, showing much love
to Mr. Goss and grief over his early death, Dr. Pratt
suddenly turned to the people and said: 'If you love
Mr. Goss render fruitful his labors in your behalf;
he tried very hard to reconcile you, but he is removed from among you before reaching the goal of
success. Now come, be reconciled to one another
around his grave; let his death be the means of a

great blessing to you.' It was done. All pride and obstinacy melted; the quarrel was buried with what was mortal of their beloved young missionary in one grave, and the alienated ones returned together loving as brethren."

2—ANOTHER INCIDENT

Reported by one of the preachers of the Cilicia Union will sufficiently explain itself:

"In September, 1866, when I was thirteen years old, I was bitten in my right foot by a snake. My father's family were then Gregorian Armenians, and, according to an old custom, I was taken to a Turkish sorcerer to be cured. This man, after reading a little, in a very low voice, muttering with his lips, blew into my mouth, and into the wound made by the snake. After he had kept this up for seven days, he found he could not cure my foot and left me to nature. I remained in that state for four months, till my foot and leg, below the knee, were wasted and decayed. When I was in that condition some Protestant neighbors brought Dr. Pratt to our house to see me. On the 18th of Janurary, 1867, he cut off the limb eight inches below the knee. To the question: 'How many piasters, sir, do you wish as your fee,' he replied, 'If you will go to school and receive an education, I shall have received my fee.' Yes, besides not accepting any

fee, he placed me, of course with my own consent,
in the Protestant school, and defrayed the expense
of my books and tuition from his own purse. I was
received into the Marash Theological Seminary the
year Dr. Pratt died, and finished my studies there
in 1878, and ever since I have, by the divine favor,
been preaching the Gospel of Christ, and desire to
continue this service till death. Yes! a poisonous
serpent was the preacher which was the occasion
of my own conversion, and of leading all my family
to Christ. I am very happy in the blessed service in
which I am employed, and I often mention in my
preaching, this incident which was the turning
point of my own life. I have been greatly impressed
by such texts as Matt. 16: 26, 18: 8, 9; John 9: 3;
Romans 8: 28. I shall never cease to recall the fact
that it was Dr. Pratt's gentleness and generosity and
unpretentious kindness that saved my body from
death, and attracted me to Christ."

XXVII

AS TEACHER.

It is difficult to say what Dr. Pratt was, rather
what he would have been, as a teacher. His other
duties were too many,—his health, in all those later
years too broken, to allow him to do himself any

sort of justice as a theological instructor. That
he had it in him to be a teacher of the highest order,
no one who knew him well could ever doubt. That
he was a successful teacher, accurate, incisive, inspiring, in Medicine, in Theology, in Science, in Language, there are those living whose lives and work,
even more than any spoken or written words will
testify. But far beyond any direct work of his, in
training either doctors or preachers, is the value of
the lesson which his whole life emphasized, viz., the
practicability and the wisdom of a thorough education of competent and consecrated native talent, in
order that the widest and the highest spheres of
usefulness in the work of elevating the several nationalities of Turkey may be, in the case of each
race, filled by the sons of that race.*

---

*It is sometimes asked, "Does it pay to attempt to educate the
youth of Turkey?" Take this simple statement of a case, paral-
leled in all its essential features hundreds of times. A bright
lad begs to be received as a day pupil into the preparatory depart-
ment of college. The family is poor; the lad cannot pay the
tuition fee; a friend assumes the responsibility, and he is received.
He steps rapidly to the head of his class. Winter approaches;
Joseph is always in his place, his eyes as keen, his face as smil-
ing, his lessons as perfect, all his behavior as blameless as ever.
But he looks pitiably thin; he still wears the same scanty summer clothing. A teacher learns that he comes to the college door
barefoot, and then puts on his shoes; poor protection against the
cold they are, but all that can be had for a long time to come.
It is manifestly time to break over the fine reserve of the worthy
poor.

"Joseph, I'm going home with you to-day." He is surprised
and silent. "Won't you take me with you?"

He recovers his courtesy, blushes and says: "Oh, yes sir, but
I'm afraid our house isn't fit to receive you."

As they walk along the snowy path together, Joseph confides
to his teacher his desire to go through college and the Theological Seminary also, and be a preacher to his people.

XXVIII.

NEARER GLIMPSES.

His friends were many; his intimate friends were few; but those he "grappled with hooks of steel." He had the rare facility of seeing and rejoicing, without reserve, in others' successes, and of show; ing that he did so by some kind, brief word. Many such instances are recalled, like the sweet echo of a "song in the night." Once, on his hearing of the death of a native brother, a preacher of the Gospel, his wife found him in his study weeping. "It is worth a whole life's labor to have been the means of saving one such soul," he said. There is a letter before the writer, which was written shortly before his first visit to America, in which he pleads for special pecuniary help from personal friends, to aid in a pressing missionary enterprise; he laments the lack of a worthy interest in the American Churches

---

Look into that house, a bare room, windows with no glass, no food or fuel; there is a loom at which a widowed sister works, earning seven cents a day. On one side sits the blind mother. In a corner the father is lying; he went away to earn something for the winter, started back with five dollars, was robbed on the way, took a violent cold and came home to die, before the winter was over. Here is a little sister, and out on the street-corners is an elder brother, a mere lad, earning five cents a day at knife-grinding.

"Why, Joseph, you'll have to stay out of school and try to earn something," the teacher said.

"My sister and brother don't want me to," he replied.

Two bread winners in a family of six, one sick, another blind, and their earnings, twelve cents a day, must meet the expense of rent, fuel, clothing, food, and send one of their number to college!

in missionary work, and expresses the conviction that lives, even in missionary homes, have been sacrificed to a too niggardly theory of expenditure; but the letter is too full of tears, was written in a confidence of family correspondence too absolute to allow being given to the public. His salary, in those first years, was $550, and it appears, from a private letter, that he used to give some $60 a year to the poor and to the work.

It is not for us to enter the inner sanctuary of his domestic life; it is enough to know that sweetness and tenderness ever blended with duty and blessed his home. We venture to make two or three extracts from his private correspondence with Dr. Farnsworth, already referred to. He writes, September 16, 1856, after the death of their first child, Nelly:

"How my heart clung to her, how bright her smile; her laugh, what a joy it was! How we would play peek-a-boo behind the door, till both were very children for laughter, I as childish as she! How she would run and nestle in my bosom, and then off again. But all is past, and only its memory remains,—and the blessed hopes."

Again, April, 1857:

"We would weep and pray together, and thank God for our angel children, your two and our two. I do thank Him. Nelly was the sunniest vision

which has crossed my path, and your little ones
were, I know, equally dear. It approaches a year
now, but that beautiful brow, and glad, bright eye
and ringing laugh are here as if I heard them now.
To what height of glory they have soared no mind
can conceive. Let us go, too, dear brother and sister;—but not now; the dross is not all purged away;
the work of God is not all done. We will wait till
then, and our angels will have grown, and when
we enter the gate, will take and bear us away right
to the throne. Then we shall praise God that they
have gone before."

There is a short, sad letter, full of pathos, of
August 5, 1858, which reveals his struggling soul,
holding on, with numb hands, in the darkness, to
the Eternal Rock, while a new wave of sorrow rolls
over him, in the death of his third child, Willie,
two days before. He also reports other sorrows
which have come over other missionary families,
and another he saw coming—Mrs. Beebee died November, 1858.

We gladly make room for the following from Miss
West:

"My reminiscences of our beloved friend and missionary brother, Dr. Pratt, are all of the most tender
and affectionate character. In his last letter, written when I was seeking rest in the home land, he in-
quired after my pecuniary needs, adding: 'We can

always manage to spare a fifty dollars for Sister Maria.' Although never requiring this aid, I was much touched by this proof of his affectionate care and thoughtfulness for me, when over-burdened himself. And he was so delicate and unostentatious in doing a kindness that it was doubly appreciated; he delighted in others' happiness, and was ever ready to bear another's burden. He was always quiet, dignified, self-contained, and one felt that there was in him a reserved force that could be drawn upon in time of need. He was utterly devoid of self-seeking, and yet did not criticise others who made themselves or their exploits the theme of conversation. He was a born gentleman; he could not stoop to do a low or mean act; he was the soul of honor, and the people trusted and loved him. They felt that he sought simply the glory of the Master and their good. He was reticent in regard to speaking of his own labors and the inner life of his own soul. He was tenderly devoted to his children, 'my house is full of blessings,' he said, and his letters reveal the depth and wealth of affection that commonly lay concealed. I give two brief extracts from his letters to me, the first of November, 1869, and the other of January, 1868:

"'Last Friday, in the evening, came along a little wee thing, and begged a place in our house and hearts, and got it. Her human name is Eliza

Macy Pratt. I don't know what the angels call her.
She is very pretty and good, and her mamma is
very quiet and happy. So you have made up your
mind to write 'a little book.' (The Romance of
Missions). Very well, I don't envy you. I have
had enough of it; a little Arithmetic, Theological
Class-book, Turkish Grammar, editing a Physiology,
a Turkish Reader—and now this great Bible work.
I am over-tasked; have not an ounce of extra
strength.

"'Did I ever tell you much of Clara? She was a
very sweet, pure, transparent, truthful, faithful
child. We could trust her anywhere. We sadly
miss her. The day before your letter came was her
birthday. How old she is now I cannot reckon, she
has gone home—blessed home!'"

It is no part of the desire or design of the writer
to represent our brother as faultless; he was a man,
and so not perfect till he passed out of our sight.
But those who knew him best would unite in saying that his character had ususual completeness and
harmony. There were no towering talents or achieve-
ments set off by equally colossal defects; no salient
faults, nothing to which truthful biography requires
the writer to give setting or permanence. He had
not commanding physical presence, but he had a
certain sparkle of mind, rarer and finer than wit or
pleasantry; his utterances were ever clear, brief, in-

cisive, effective. He was not a man of assumption, but one was not encouraged to trench, a second time, on what was his clear prerogative.

On one occasion he was talking with a younger associate about a missionary question in the settlement of which much was made, in certain quarters, of the feelings, or amour-prope, of certain brethren. Turning round in his quick, incisive way, he said: ' Brother ——, whenever you have any question of Christian duty to consider and decide, just put your feelings in your pockets.'

———

XXIX.

WEIGHT OF JUDGMENT AND BREADTH OF SCHOLARSHIP

Dr. Pratt went to Constantinople for a specific work, but he was a member of the Missionary Station, and the soundness of his judgment and the breadth of his experience in all phases of missionary work, had this natural result that his advice was much sought, and his judgment had great weight in connection with the perplexing questions then arising.

This was also true in affairs concerning Robert College, near which he resided; and had he lived and enjoyed even the tolerable health of his later years, he would have been called, probably, to a profes-

sor's chair in the college. And, after finishing the
work of Bible translation, he would doubtless have
accepted a position in the college. He could have
filled such a position, while he would have been
unequal to the physical strain of resuming the mul-
tifarious and continuous burdens of work in his old
and loved field, south of the Taurus mountains.

His fitness for a professorship in more than one
branch of natural science, in philology or meta-
physics was well known. One brochure of his, in
philology was published, years ago, by the American Oriental Society. It was on the Turkish language, and the different alphabets in which it is
written.

XXX.

RELATION OF A LIFE TO ITS RESULTS.

Our brother was a man of enthusiasm in the best
sense of the word, not the enthusiasm that dashes to
the front, assumes responsibilities and compromises
others, but the enthusiasm of hard, steady, silent
work, without trumpet-blowing—which he detested
—in the glowing confidence that God will care for
all the issues. While, with a lively faith, he looked
for "immediate and tangible results" of work done
—and saw them—he never forgot that an enduring
spiritual structure can be built only on solid foun-

dations; he was patient with the necessary work of clearing away rubbish, and finding, or making, something solid on which to lay the foundation stones, whether in ecclesiastical or educational work. In the city of Damascus, builders have sometimes to dig through debris thirty feet thick before they can find the solid earth. He had that robustness of faith and of spiritual fibre that accepts the conditions necessary for the largest and most lasting spiritual results, even if those results should lie beyond the life-span of one generation of workers.

Growth in the evangelical work in Turkey, since his day has been marked, steady and in all directions. The salient points are mainly these, viz:

1. The development of intelligent, self-reliant, manly, Christian character, in the more than three hundred evangelical communities, manifesting itself in an earnest and intelligent assuming, by native Christians, of the responsibility of sustaining and administering their own institutions; and

2. In a demand for and appreciation of higher Christian education, not only among Protestants but almost equally among Armenians and Greeks which has led us to establish colleges and high schools · for both sexes, and is filling them with paying pupils.

These Evangelical Christian Institutions hold the leadership in education in all Western Asia, and

have already proved to be those foci about which
are organizing the several interests that, at one
time, threatened to disintegrate, and imperil the
future of Christian unity. These institutions are
drawing the sympathies of all Christian races, and
making them accessible to evangelical influence. To
the philanthropist as he examines the outlook in
Western Asia, they are the beacon lights—electric
lights—upon the hilltops. In their light we hope
and we trust that no influence hostile to vital Christianity will be permitted to dominate the re-awak-
ening life of the races of Asia Minor amid impend-
ing changes.

XXXI.

THE CLOSING SCENES.

After all the years of weakness through which
our brother had passed, one might almost think that
no summons to enter the rest and service of the
heavenly life could be either unexpected or unwel-
come. And while he did lay down his work in the
same spirit in which he had taken it up twenty
years before, viz.: in obedience to the personal call
of the Lord of the harvest, yet it is certain that it
was with feelings of disappointment that he learned
that he had an incurable disease, and that his re-
maining days were few. He loved the ministry of

Christ's Gospel in this world; he gladly anticipated the fulfillment of prophecy concerning the spread and triumph of the Redeemer's Kingdom, and in his regard, most blessed are they who are its heralds.

Rev. Prof. A. L. Long, D.D., of Robert College, has kindly communicated the following:

"From my first acquaintance with Dr. Pratt, a close and brotherly intimacy was commenced between us, which continued unbroken until I closed his eyes as he passed away from earth. I had exceptional opportunities for studying his inner life and character. We were alone together when the fatal discovery was made, revealing the hopeless character of the malady from which he had been, for some time, suffering. I was present when the consulting physicians endeavored to encourage him and to rally his nervous energies to a struggle for life. He submitttd gently, pleasantly, courteously: but his own professional knowledge prevented him from being convinced by their arguments. After his medical advisers had left him, I asked him if there was anything I could do for him. 'There is,' said he, grasping my hand warmly; 'I want you to stay by me until the end.' From that hour till 'the end,' which came in about six weeks, I was at his bedside or within call, all the time save the regular hours devoted to my classes in the college.

We talked much together during this time. Our topics of conversation were of the same general character as that to which we had been accustomed in former times. We talked of scientific discoveries, of biology, of archeology, of philology, in all of which he took great interest, and had amassed large stores of information. We talked also of the loving Savior, the nature of personal religion, and the blessedness of a firm, unfaltering trust in Christ, and of a personal experience of his pardoning love. Then we talked of the prospects of the Gospel in these Oriental lands, and some of the special troubles, which about that time were trying the hearts of the missionary brethren and all the friends of missions in these lands. Those were blessed hours of sweet brotherly converse. Through the whole of that period of suffering, he was the same thoughtful, patient, gentle, Christian scholar. While there was no rapturous demonstration of joy, there was a trust which never for a moment faltered; and as his feet touched the icy stream, and he bade me an affectionate farewell, there was upon his countenance that expression of holy peace and calm which testified of the sustaining presence of Him who hath conquered death and the grave. I felt that the chamber where this 'good man met his fate,' was truly a privileged place, and that my own faith was strengthened by the experience of that hour. Years

have passed, but his memory is fresh and green in
my heart, and I cherish the recollection of my association with him among the most precious of the
experiences of my life."

President Washburn of Robert College says:

"He contemplated death with perfect calmness
and perfect resignation, and we sang at his funeral
the chant, 'Thy Will be Done,' which I had heard
him sing by himself with a depth of feeling that I
can never forget."

He died December 5, 1872, in the forty-seventh
year of his age, at his home at Roumeli Hissar, and
his remains were quietly laid to rest, as he would
have chosen, in the Protestant cemetery at Feri-
keny, outside of Pera, on the north, on a height west
of the Bosphorus, where, with some who wrought
in the same work before him, with many members
of missionary families, he awaits the final reunion
of the one family of God.

SUGGESTIVE BOOKS - -
- - FOR BIBLE READERS.

NEW NOTES FOR BIBLE READINGS. By the late S. R. BRIGGS, with brief Memoir of the author by Rev. JAS. H. BROOKES, D. D., Crown 8vo, cloth, $1.00; flexible, 75 cents.

"NEW NOTES" is not a reprint, and contains *Bible Readings* to be found in no other similar work, and, it is confidently believed, will be found more carefully prepared, and therefore more helpful and suggestive.

Everyone of the 60,000 readers of "Notes and Suggestions for Bible Readings" will welcome this entirely new collection containing selections from D. L. Moody, Major Whittle, J. H. Brookes, D. D., Prof. W. G. Moorehead, Rev. E. P. Marvin, Jno. Currie, Rev. W. J Erdman, Rev. F. E. Marsh, Dr. L. W. Munhall, etc.

NOTES AND SUGGESTIONS FOR BIBLE READINGS. By S. R. BRIGGS and J. H. ELLIOTT.

Containing, in addition to twelve introductory chapters on plans and method of Bible study and Bible readings, over six hundred outlines of Bible readings, by many of the most eminent Bible students of the day. Crown 8vo, 262 pp. Cloth, library style, $1.00; flexible cloth, .75; paper covers, .50.

THE OPEN SECRET; or, The Bible Explaining Itself. A series of intensely practical Bible readings. By HANNAH WHITALL SMITH. 320 pp. Fine cloth, $1.00.

That the author of this work has a faculty of presenting the "Secret Things" that are revealed in the Word of God is apparent to all who have read the exceedingly popular work, "The Christian's Secret of a Happy Life."

BIBLE BRIEFS; or, Outline Themes for Scripture Students. By G. C. & E. A. NEEDHAM. 16mo., 224 pages, cloth, $1.00.

The plan of these expositions is suggestive rather than exhaustive, and these suggestions are designed to aid Evangelists at home and missionaries abroad, Bible School Teachers, and Christian Association Secretaries and Workers.

BIBLE HELPS FOR BUSY MEN. By A. C. P. COOTE.

Contains over 200 Scripture subjects, clearly worked out and printed in good legible type, with an alphabetical index. 140 pages, 16mo.; paper, 40c.; cloth flex., 60c.
"Likely to be of use to overworked brethren."—C. H. SPURGEON.
"Given in a clear and remarkably telling form."—*Christian Leader.*

RUTH, THE MOABITESS; or Gleaning in the Book of Ruth. By HENRY MOORHOUSE. 16mo., paper covers, 20c.; cloth, 40c.

A characteristic series of Bible readings, full of suggestion and instruction.

BIBLE READINGS. By HENRY MOORHOUSE. 16mo., paper covers, 30 cents; cloth, 60 cents.

A series by one pre-eminently the man of one book, an incessant, intense, prayerful student of the Bible.

SYMBOLS AND SYSTEMS IN BIBLE READINGS. Rev. W. F. CRAFTS. 64 pages and cover, 25 cents.

Giving a plan of Bible reading, with fifty verses definitely assigned for each day, the Bible being arranged in the order of its events. The entire symbolism of the Bible explained concisely and clearly.

NEW YORK:
12 Bible House, Astor Pl. Fleming H. Revell CHICAGO:
148 & 150 Madison St.

REFERENCE BOOKS
FOR
BIBLE STUDENTS.

JAMIESON, FAUSSET & BROWN'S Popular Portable Commentary. Critical, Practical, Explanatory. Four volumns in neat box, fine cloth, $8.00; half bound, $10.00.

A new edition, containing the complete unabridged notes in clear type on good paper, in four handsome 12 mo. volumes of about 1.000 pages each, with copious index, numerous illustrations and maps, and a Bible Dictionary compiled from Dr. Wm. Smith's standard work.

Bishop Vincent of Chautauqua fame says : " The *best* condensed commentary on the whole Bible is Jamieson, Fausset & Brown.''

CRUDEN'S UNABRIDGED CONCORDANCE TO THE HOLY SCRIPTURES. With life of the author. 864 pp., 8vo., cloth (net), $1.00 ; half roan, sprinkled edges (net), 2.00 ; half roan, full gilt edges (net), $2.50.

SMITH'S BIBLE DICTIONARY, comprising its Antiquities, Biography, Geography and Natural History, with numerous maps and illustrations. Edited and condensed from his great work by WILLIAM SMITH, LL. D. 776 pages, 8vo, many illustrations, cloth, $1.50.

THE BIBLE TEXT CYCLOPEDIA. A complete classification of Scripture Texts in the form of an alphabetical list of subjects. By Rev. JAMES INGLIS. Large 8vo, 524 pages, cloth, $1.75.

The plan is much the same as the " Bible Text Book'' with the valuable additional help in that the texts referred to are quoted in full. Thus the student is saved the time and labor of turning to numerous passages, which, when found, may not be pertinent to the subject he has in hand.

THE TREASURY OF SCRIPTURE KNOWLEDGE ; consisting of 500,000 scripture references and parallel passages, with numerous notes. 8vo, 778 pages. cloth, $2.00.

A single examination of this remarkable compilation of references will convince the reader of the fact that '' the Bible is its own best interpreter.''

THE WORKS OF FLAVIUS JOSEPHUS, translated by WILLIAM WHISTON, A. M., with Life, Portrait, Notes and Index. A new cheap edition in clear type. Large 8vo, 684 pages, cloth, $2.00.

100.000 SYNONYMS AND ANTONYMS. By Rt. Rev. SAMUEL FALLOWS, A. M., D. D. 512 pages, cloth, $1.00.

A complete Dictionary of synonyms *and words of opposite* meanings, with an appendix of Briticisms, Americanisms, Colloquialisms, Homonims, Homophonous words, Foreign Phrases, etc., etc.

" This is one of the best books of its kind we have seen, and probably there is nothing published in the country that is equal to it."—*Y. M. C. A. Watchman.*

New Books for — — Thinking Minds.

WHAT ARE WE TO BELIEVE? or, The Testimony of Fulfilled Prophecy. By Rev. JOHN URQUHART. 16mo., 230 pages, cloth, 75 cents.

" This book, so small in bulk but so large in thought, sets forth a great mass of such testimony in lines so clear and powerful that we pity the man who could read it without amazement and awe. It is the very book to put into the hands of an intelligent Agnostic."
—*The Christian*, London.

MANY INFALLIBLE PROOFS. By Rev. A. T. PIERSON, D.D. Revised Edition. 12mo, 317 pages, cloth, $1.00 ; paper, 35 cents, net.

" It is not an exercise in mental gymnastics, but an earnest inquiry after the truth."—*Daily Telegram*, Troy, N. Y.
" He does not believe that the primary end of the Bible is to teach science ; but he argues with force and full conviction that nothing in the Bible has been shaken by scientific research."—*Independent*.

HOW I REACHED THE MASSES; Together with twenty-two lectures delivered in the Birmingham Town Hall on Sunday afternoons. By Rev. CHARLES LEACH, F. G. S. 16mo., cloth, $1.00.

There is much of very welcome good sense and practical illustration in these addresses. Pithy and pointed in admonishment, and wholesome in their didactic tone, they ought to exercise a good influence.

ENDLESS BEING; or, Man Made for Eternity. By Rev. J. L. BARLOW. Introduction by the Rev. P. S. HENSON, D. D. Cloth, 16mo., 165 pages, 75 cents.

An unanswerable work ; meeting the so-called annihilation and kindred theories most satisfactorily. The author held for years these errors, and writes as one fully conversant with the ground he covers. It is a work which should be widely circulated.

PAPERS ON PREACHING. By the Right Rev. Bishop BALDWIN, Rev. Principal RAINY, D. D., Rev. J. R. VERNON, M. A., and others. Crown, 8vo, cloth, 75 cents.

" Preachers of all denominations will do well to read these practical and instructive disquisitions. The essay on " Expression in Preaching " is especially good.—*Christian*.

THE SABBATH; its Permanence, Promise, and Defence. By Rev. W. W. EVERTS, D. D. 12mo., 278 pages, cloth, $1.00.

No phase of the Sabbath question is left undiscussed, while every topic is treated in the briefest manner, and every touch of light shows the hand of a master.
" An incisive and effective discussion of the subject."—*N. Y. Observer*.
" A thoughtful Christian defence of that divine institution."—*Christian Advocate*.

QUESTIONS OF THE AGES. By Rev. MOSES SMITH. Cloth 12mo, 132 pages, 75 cents.

What is the Almighty?	*Is there Common Sense in Religion?*
What is man?	*What is Faith?*
What is the Trinity?	*Is there a Larger Hope?*
Which is the Great Commandment.	*Is Life Worth Living?*

What Mean these Stones?

" Discusses certain of the deep things of the Gospel in such a wise and suggestive fashion that they are helpful. One, answers negatively and conclusively the question, Is there a larger hope? '—*The Congregationalist*.

◁HAND BOOKS FOR BIBLE STUDENTS▷

THE LIFE OF CHRIST. Rev. JAS. STALKER, M. A. A new edition, with introduction by Rev. GEO. C. LORIMER, D. D. 12mo. cloth, 166 pages, 60 cents.

This work is in truth "*Multum in Parvo,*" containing within small compass a vast amount of most helpful teaching, so admirably arranged that the reader gathers with remarkable definiteness the whole revealed record of the life work of our Lord in a nutshell of space and with a minimum of study.

THE LIFE OF ST. PAUL. By Rev. JAS. STALKER, M. A. 12mo. cloth, 184 pages, 60 cents.

As admirable a work as the exceedingly popular volume by this author on "The Life of Christ."

"An exceedingly compact life of the Apostle to the Gentiles. It is bristling with information, and is brief, yet clear. As an outline of Paul's life it cannot be surpassed."— *N. Y. Christian Inquirer.*

THE BIBLE STUDENTS' HANDBOOK. 12mo cloth, 288 pages, 50 cents.

One of those helpful works, worth its price, multiplied by several scores. It contains an introduction to the study of the Scriptures, with a brief account of the books of the Bible, their writers, etc., also a synopsis of the life and work of our Lord, and complete history of the manners and customs of the times, etc.

THE TOPICAL TEXT BOOK. 16mo. cloth, 292 pages, 60 cents.

A remarkably complete and helpful Scripture text book for the topical study of the Bible. Useful in preparing Bible readings, addresses, etc.

THE BIBLE REMEMBRANCER. 24mo. cloth, 198 pages, 50 cts.

A complete analyses of the Bible is here given, in small compass, in addition to a large amount of valuable Biblical information, and twelve colored maps.

BIBLE LESSONS ON JOSHUA AND JUDGES. By Rev. J. GURNEY HOARE, M. A. 16mo cloth, 124 pages, 50 cents.

FIFTY-TWO LESSONS ON (1) The Works of Our Lord; (2) Claims of Our Lord. Forming a year's course of instruction for Bible classes, Sunday schools and lectures. By FLAVEL S. COOK, M. A., D. D. 16mo. cloth, 104 pages, 50 cents.

FIFTY-TWO LESSONS ON (1) The Names and Titles of Our Lord; (2) Prophesies Concerning Our Lord and their Fulfillment. By FLAVEL S. COOK, M. A., D. D. 16mo. cloth, 104 pages, 50 cents.

Extremely full in the matter of reference and explanation, and likely to make the user "search the Scriptures."

OUTLINE OF THE BOOKS OF THE BIBLE. By Rev. J. H. BROOKES, D. D. Invaluable to the young student of the Bible as a "First Lesson" in the study of the Book. 180 pages. Cloth, 50 cents, paper covers, 25 cents.

CHRIST AND THE SCRIPTURES. By Rev. ADOLPH SAPHER. 16mo. cloth, 160 pages, 75 cents.

To all disciples of Christ this work commends itself at once by its grasp of truth, its insight, the life in it, and its spiritual force.—*Christian Work.*

WORKS OF D. L. MOODY.

By the strenuous cultivation of his gift Mr. Moody has attained to a clear and in cisive style which preachers ought to study; and he has the merit, which many more cul tivated men lack, of saying nothing that does not tend to the enforcement of the particu lar truth he is enunciating. He knows how to disencumber his text of all extraneous matter, and exhibits his wisdom as a preacher hardly less by what he leaves out than by what he includes. Apart from its primary purpose each of these books has a distinct value as a lesson on homiletics to ministers and students.—*The Christian Leader.*

Bible Characters.

Prevailing Prayer; What Hinders It. Thirtieth Thousand

To the Work! To the Work! A Trumpet Call. Thir- tieth Thousand.

The Way to God and How to Find It. One Hundred and Fifth Thousand.

Heaven; its Hope; its Inhabitants; its Happiness; its Riches; its Reward. One Hundred and Twenty-Fifth Thousand.

Secret Power ; or the Secret of Success in Christian Life and Work. Seventy-Second Thousand.

Twelve Select Sermons. One Hundred and Sixty-Fifth Thousand.

The above are bound in uniform style and price. Paper covers 30 cents: cloth, 60 cents. Also issued in cloth, beveled edge, and put up in neat box containing the seven volumes. Price of set, $4 20.

Daniel, the Prophet. Tenth Thousand. Paper cover, 20c. cloth, 40c.

The Full Assurance of Faith. Seventh Thousand. Some thoughts on Christian confidence. Paper cover, 15c.; cloth, 25c.

The Way and the Word. Sixty-Fifth Thousand. . Com- prising "Regeneration," and "How to Study the Bible." Cloth, 25c.; paper, 15c.

How to Study the Bible. Forty-Fifth Thousand. Cloth, 15c. paper, 10c.

The Second Coming of Christ. Forty-Fifth Thousand. Paper, 10c.

Inquiry Meetings. By Mr. Moody and Maj. Whittle. Paper, 15c.

Gospel Booklets. By D. L. Moody. 12 separate sermons.

Published in small square form, suitable for distribution, or inclosing in letters. 35 cents per dozen, $2.50 per hundred. May be had assorted or of any separate tract.

Any of the above sent postpaid to any address on receipt of price. Special rates for distribution made known on application.

CHICAGO: 148 & 150 Madison St. Fleming H. Revell. NEW YORK: 12 Bible House, Astor Pl.

·MISSIONARY PUBLICATIONS·

REPORT OF THE CENTENARY CONFERENCE on the Protestant Missions of the World. Held in London, June, 1888. Edited by the Rev. JAMES JOHNSTON, F. S. S., Secretary of the Conference. Two large 8vo. vols., 1200 pages, $2.00 net per set.

An important feature in this report, lack of which has prejudiced many against reports in general, is the special care taken by the Editor, who has succeeded in making the work an interesting and accurate reproduction of the most important accumulation of facts from the Mission Fields of the World, as given by the representatives of all the Evangelical Societies of Christendom.

And another: The exceptionally complete and helpful indexing of the entire work in such a thorough manner as to make it of the greatest value as a Reference Encyclopedia on mission topics for years to come.

THE MISSIONARY YEAR BOOK FOR 1889-90. Containing Historical and Statistical accounts of the Principle Protestant Missionary Societies in America, Great Britain and the Continent of Europe.

The American edition, edited by Rev. J. T. GRACEY, D.D., of Buffalo, embraces about 450 pages, one-fourth being devoted to the work of American Societies, and will contain Maps of India, China Japan, Burmah, and Siam; also a language Map of India and comparative diagrams illustrating areas, population and progress of Mission work. This compilation will be the best presentation of the work of the American Societies in Pagan Lands that has yet been given to the public. The book is strongly recommended by Rev. JAS. JOHNSTON, F.S.S., as a companion volume to the Report of the Century Conference on Missions. Cloth, 12mo. $1.25.

GARENGANZE: or, Seven Years' Pioneer Missionary Work in Central Africa. By FRED. S. ARNOT, with introduction by Rev. A. T. PIERSON, D.D. Twenty Illustrations and an original Map.

The author's two trips across Africa, entirely unarmed and unattended except by the local and constantly changing carriers, and in such marked contrast with many modern adventurers, strongly impress one to ask if another Livingstone has not appeared among us. Traversing where no white man had ever been seen before, and meeting kings and chiefs accustomed only to absolute power, he demanded and received attention in the name of his God. Cloth 8vo, 290 pages, $1.25.

IN THE FAR EAST: China Illustrated. Letters from Geraldine Guinness. Edited by her sister, with Introduction by Rev. J. HUDSON TAYLOR. A characteristic Chinese cover. Cloth 4to, 138 pages, $1.50.

CONTENTS.

"Good-Bye!"
Second Class.
On the Way to China.
Hong-Kong and Shanghai.
First days in the Flowery Land
Opium Suicides amongst Women.

Ten Days on a Chinese Canal.
At Home in our Chinese "Haddon Hall."
By Wheelbarrow to Antong.
Life on a Chinese Farm.
A Visit to the "Shun" City.
Blessing—and Need of Blessing—In the Far East.

Rev. C. H. SPURGEON, writes:

"I have greatly enjoyed 'In the Far East.' God blessing it, the book should send armies of believers to invade the Flowry Land."

The author is to be congratulated for the taste and beauty with which these letters are now put into permanent form. A full page colored map of China enhances this admirable gift book.

Popular Missionary Biographies.

12mo, 160 pages. Fully illustrated; cloth extra, 75 cents each.

Rev. C. H. SPURGEON, writes:

"Crowded with facts that both interest and inspire, we can conceive of no better plan to spread the Missionary spirit than the multiplying of such biographies; and we would specially commend this series to those who have the management of libraries and selection of prizes in our Sunday Schools."

From *The Missionary Herald*:

"We commended this series in our last issue, and a further examination leads us to renew our commendation, and to *urge* the placing of this series of missionary books in all our Sabbath-school libraries.

These books are handsomely printed and bound and are beautifully illustrated, and we are confident that they will prove attractive to all young people."

SAMUEL CROWTHER, the Slave Boy who became Bishop of the Niger. By JESSE PAGE, author of "Bishop Patterson."

THOMAS J. COMBER, Missionary Pioneer to the Congo. By Rev. J. B. MYERS, Association Secretary Baptist Missionary Society.

BISHOP PATTESON, the Martyr of Melanesia. By JESSE PAGE.

GRIFFITH JOHN, Founder of the Hankow Mission, Central China. By WM. ROBSON, of the London Missionary Society.

ROBERT MORRISON, the Pioneer of Chinese Missions. By WM. J. TOWNSEND, Sec. Methodist New Connexion Missionary Soc'y.

ROBERT MOFFAT, the Missionary Hero of Kuruman. By DAVID J. DEANE, author of "Martin Luther, the Reformer," etc.

WILLIAM CAREY, the Shoemaker who became a Missionary. By Rev. J. B. MYERS, Association Secretary Baptist Missionary Society.

JAMES CHALMERS, Missionary and Explorer of Rarotonga and New Guinea. By WM. ROBSON, of the London Missionary Soc'y.

MISSIONARY LADIES IN FOREIGN LANDS. By Mrs. E. R. PILMAN, author of "Heroines of the Mission Fields," etc.

JAMES CALVERT; or, From Dark to Dawn in Fiji.

JOHN WILLIAMS, the Martyr of Erromanga. By Rev. JAMES J. ELLIS.

UNIFORM WITH THE ABOVE.

THE WORLD'S BENEFACTORS.

JOHN BRIGHT, the Man of the People. By JESSE PAGE, author of "Bishop Patteson," "Samuel Crowther," etc.

HENRY M. STANLEY, the African Explorer. By ARTHUR MONTEFIORE, F.R.G.S. Brought down to 1889.

DAVID LIVINGSTONE, the Pioneer of the Dark Continent.

NEW YORK:
12 Bible House, Astor Pl.
Fleming H. Revell
CHICAGO:
148 & 150 Madison St.

FOR WORK AMONG CHILDREN.

Attractive Truths in Lesson and Story. By Mrs. A. M. SCUDDER, with introduction by Rev. F. E CLARKE, Prest. Y. P. S. C. E. 12 mo; cloth, $1 25.

A series of outline lessons with illustrative stories for Junior Christian Endeavor Societies, for Children's meetings and for home teaching.

Not only for workers among children will this work be appreciated, but mothers will find it a delightful Sunday afternoon volume for their children, suggesting an endless variety of "occupations," besides charming with its many beautiful stories.

Children's Meetings and How to Conduct Them. By LUCY J. RIDER, and NELLIE M. CARMAN, introduction by Bishop J. H. VINCENT. 208 pp., cloth, illustrated, $1 00; paper covers, 50 cents.

"Mr. Revell has conferred a favor on the Christian public, especially that large part of it interested in the right training of children, in publishing this most practical work."—*The Advance.*

"Just such a work as teachers have long wanted. It will at once take a place among the indispensables."—*N. Y. Observer.*

"Among the contributors to this volume are nearly all the best known Sunday-school writers of this country. The book is a cyclopedia of helpful hints on the best plans of working among the children, plans suggested by the actual experience of the contributors."

Clear as Crystal. By Rev. R. T. CROSS. Fifty, five minute talks on lessons from Crystals. 206 pp., beveled cloth, $1 00.

"The Sermons belong to the five minute series, and are *models* of what can be done in so brief a space."—*The Independent*

"Most interesting in style, *and full of spirituality*. We commend this volume especially to teachers who understand the value of fresh illustrations from nature."—*The Christian at Work.*

Talks to Children. By Rev. T. T. EATON, D. D., with introduction by Rev. JOHN A. BROADUS, D. D., LL. D. 16 mo. cloth, $1 00.

"Dr. Eaton's *Talks* appear to us to possess *in an unusual degree* the qualities which interest and profit young hearers and readers. They reproduce Scripture history in the terms of modern life and give it both a vivid setting before the youthful imagination, and a firm grip on the youthful conscience."—*The Independent.*

"We have examined this work with intense interest. We have read many books of this kind, *but we honestly believe that this volume of Dr. Eaton's excels them all.*"—*Central Baptist.*

"The *best* book of the kind we remember to have seen. We commend it especially to parents reading aloud to their children Sunday afternoon."—*Examiner.*

Short Talks to Young Christians, on the Evidences of Christianity. By Rev. C. O. BROWN. 168 pages, cloth, 50c., paper, 30 cents.

"Books that are really useful, on the evidences of Christianity, could almost be counted on one's fingers. One which has been singled out from a host of others by its plain straight forward sense is 'Short Talks to Young Christians on the Evidences'. by the Rev. C. O. BROWN."—*Sunday School Times.*

Conversion of Children. By Rev. E. P. HAMMOND. A practical volume replete with incident and illustration. Suggestive, important and timely. 184 pages, cloth, 75 cents, paper cover, 30 cents.

Young People's Christian Manual. By Rev. CHAS L. MORGAN. 32mo. booklet, 5 cents; 25 copies, $1 00.

A Catechetical Manual for the instruction of the young for use in Pastors' Training Classes, Societies of Christian Endeavor, Sunday School, or Family.

"I have for years felt the need of something of this sort. I wish the Manual might be wanted as widely as I am sure it is needed."—*Josiah Strong, D. D., author "Our Country."*

NEW YORK: 12 Bible House, Astor Pl. Fleming H. Revell, CHICAGO: 148 & 150 Madison St.

www.ingramcontent.com/pod-product-compliance
Lightning Source LLC
Chambersburg PA
CBHW020030030726
47499CB00007B/2349